Maid
of the
King's Court

Maid of the King's Court

Lucy Worsley

CANDLEWICK PRESS

Copyright © 2016 by Lucy Worsley

First U.S. edition 2017
First published as *Eliza Rose* by Bloomsbury Publishing (U.K.) 2016

Library of Congress Catalog Card Number pending
ISBN 978-0-7636-8806-6

16 17 18 19 20 21 BVG 10 9 8 7 6 5 4 3 2 1

Printed in Berryville, VA, U.S.A.

This book was typeset in Celestia Antiqua MVB.

Candlewick Press
99 Dover Street
Somerville, Massachusetts 02144

visit us at www.candlewick.com

To Kersti Worsley

Contents

Part One: At Stoneton Castle

Part Two: At Trumpton Hall

Part Three: At Court

Part Four: To the Tower

Part One

At Stoneton Castle

Chapter 1

Today You Must Become a Woman

6 NOVEMBER 1535
ELIZABETH IS TWELVE...

I'd always known that my adult life would begin once I was twelve. And that this would mean marriage.

Aunt Margaret had been working hard to prepare me.

"Duty, Elizabeth," she used to say, thumping her walking cane down with every word, with every step. "It is your duty to be a good daughter and, when your father has arranged a suitable alliance, it is your duty to be an obliging wife. You must be ready."

Duty. A word as heavy as the thickest featherbed.

I would often lie in bed, wondering about my future husband. A prince? A knight? A duke? A stable boy? Of course, the last was a wicked fancy. Aunt Margaret often said I had the devil in me on account of my wild nature and red hair. I was inordinately proud of my long, red hair. I'd heard it was the same colour as the king's own and that of his daughter, the Princess Elizabeth. I wondered if they were plagued like me with blotchy freckles across my rather beaky nose.

"Of course you're not a beauty," Aunt Margaret used to say, "but it's the bloodline that counts. Our family is one of the oldest in Derbyshire." So naturally I couldn't marry anyone I wanted. My father would make me a match into a family at least equal to ours in dignity and antiquity.

It was all very well to mull over whether I would rather be a princess or a duchess while safely tucked up in bed. But when Henny, my nurse, shook me awake on the November morning of my twelfth birthday, goose pimples spread all over my skin even before she had pulled back the slightly mangy fur coverlet.

"Hurry up, child," Henny said. "Your father wishes to speak to you."

I began to yawn and stretch myself, but suddenly the thought of the cold was banished from my mind. "Henny!" I said urgently. "Have you forgotten what day it is?"

"It's Tuesday, my love," she said, now with her back to me, pulling down the blanket we pegged over the window to keep out the worst of the draught at night.

"Henny!"

Her shoulders twitched. An instant too late I realised that of course she knew perfectly well that today was my birthday. She turned round with a broad smile.

"Gah!" I said, making a fist and tugging at my long braid. She had caught me out. But I could not help grinning back. A new thought struck me as I tossed my messy plait back over my shoulder. "Henny, does my father want to give me a present?"

"I don't think so, not at this hour." My father wasn't very good at remembering things like presents anyway. But Henny could be relied upon to have got me a sugar mouse or a new pair of velvet slippers.

"Well, what then?"

"What a question! As if his lordship would discuss such a thing with me."

I laughed. "Oh, Henny, he knows you're one of our family!"

"Nonsense, child. Now hurry." She turned away quickly as if to stir up the miserable little fire in our great, gaping stone hearth. But she was too late and I'd detected that she was beaming.

Henny was my nurse, but really I was far too grown-up to need one. I called her instead my "tiring woman," who helped me to get dressed or attired. Unfortunately, Henny herself kept forgetting about her new status, and when I reminded her, she would usually say that I was the tiring one, and that I quite wore her out with my questions, my constant demands for new stories ("not *that* one, we had it last week"), and the mess that I made of my clothes.

Despite Henny's efforts with the fire, it was so cold that the tiny glass panes of my window were beaded with moisture. I snatched my toes back from the freezing floor and burrowed round in my bed for a pair of woollen stockings I had taken off last night. It had been too chilly to get out of my bed to return them to their proper place in the chest. As I threw off the coverlet and the rather threadbare linen sheets, Henny handed me my heavy velvet robe with the fur trim. It was a sumptuous garment that was sadly disfigured by a great stain down the front. Nothing in our house, Stoneton — a snake of ancient grey towers running along the top of a hill — was quite as grand as it seemed at first.

I did up my robe as quickly as I could. Catching a glimpse of freezing fog outside the window, I grabbed a shawl to go on top. I had hardly finished swathing myself in fabric when Henny prodded me towards the door. "All right, all right!" I grumbled. There was never usually this level of urgency in our early morning routine, even on a birthday.

Henny shooed me down the uneven floor of the long gallery, and we passed by the door to the best bedchamber. It always stood empty, being saved for important guests who never came. Next to it hung a tapestry showing a forest in full leaf, which actually concealed a tiny little hidden door. This led to the sally port, the secret staircase, and my favourite part of our house. The winding steps led upwards to the walkway that led around the high defensive walls, and downwards they took you to the hidden entrance from the garden. I would often steal away to the secret stairs myself, looking for a place to hide when my father was in a bad temper. Henny spotted my hesitation by the secret door.

"You're not in trouble this morning, you know," she said, giving my shoulder a little squeeze.

I shook her off impatiently. I quite often *was* in trouble, for making a smart answer or failing to keep my things tidy, and then the sally port became my refuge. Running down those stairs, I would pretend I was a knight like Prince Arthur of old, clanking in my spurs, ready to repel invaders. Running up them, I liked to reach the wall walk, and then climb to the top of our highest tower, imagining that all the land in every direction was my own.

It would have been, once upon a time, but the farms had been sold and forests felled. Indeed, in the middle of what should have been our finest hunting park, a trembling column of grey smoke arose from the lead smelting concern that my father had set up with capital he could ill afford, and which had yet to produce any of the money we desperately needed.

Aunt Margaret constantly complained that we never had the kind of feasts and balls that she and my father had enjoyed in their youth. This was because of the Great Forfeit, which had been paid by my father's long-dead elder brother, the traitor Baron Camperdowne. But if I ever asked about him, she told me for the hundredth time that a maid should be seen and not heard.

The early hour, the unexpected summons, and Henny's brusque kindness gave me a disturbing sense that something important was about to happen. I felt a little hollow inside. It had been a long time since last night's pottage and bread, and that had hardly been a feast. I dug my fingers into my palms to keep my hands from twitching with nerves. At Henny's nod, I knocked on the door to the Great Chamber.

Inside were huge windows cut into walls hung

with faded tapestries. Along one side of the room ran black-stained wooden panelling, from which the white painted faces of our ancestors peered down. I knew that they were watching and judging me. My grandfather was there in the line-up, and my mother, but one portrait was missing. There was a blank patch in the corner where Aunt Margaret had had a picture removed. My traitor uncle.

My father was standing at the window when I entered, his warm breath misting the glass.

His name was Lord Anthony Camperdowne, and he was the Baron of Stone. It was because he had no sons that Aunt Margaret was constantly drumming it into me that one day I would have to take on the responsibility for our great grey house of Stoneton. I knew that it was a very old and very important house, and that our family was very old and important too. But my father did not look important. He was a thin, wiry, short man, with a pointed little ginger beard and baggy breeches. He sometimes reminded me of a fox, his head constantly swivelling round in search of danger or opportunity. Now he swivelled it towards me and smiled.

"Elizabeth," he said, gesturing to me to join him near the window.

As I crossed the rush matting, I looked at him carefully. His face was creased and worried. He often looked like that in the morning when he had played cards all night with our very rare visitors to Stoneton. It was a warning to me that he might be in the mood when even a simple question would meet a barked demand for silence.

"Father, are you well?" I asked cautiously, not daring to mention my birthday.

"Quite well, thank you. This is a great day." Despite his cheerful words, I noticed a catch in his voice, and he turned back to look out of the window. I thought that he must be observing the broken pane in the corner, where the wind whistled in, but then I saw that his gaze had drifted out farther over to the fields in the distance. "Today you must become a woman."

I was a woman already, I reminded myself, two years into double figures, and with a tiring woman of my own. I felt a little indignant that he had forgotten and threw back my shoulders. At the same time, though, a pinprick of anxiety and curiosity had started up in my empty stomach. My father was still staring out the window, and the silence began to drag. I opened my mouth to ask him what he meant but thought the better of it.

"This day," he said at last, "I will accept the Earl of Westmorland's offer. You are to be wed to his son. Does that make you happy?"

For a second or two, I could not think what I ought to say. My hands seemed to have crept of their own accord across my belly to comfort each other. Then it came to me.

"Of course, Father," I said. I lifted the skirt of my gown, bobbing down and bowing my head submissively, just as Aunt Margaret had taught me. Inside, though, my stomach felt wobbly. I knew that I would have to marry, for the good of my family, but I hadn't realised it would be quite so soon.

"Happy? What has happiness got to do with it?"

The voice came from the doorway. I turned and saw Aunt Margaret standing there, black as a crow against the daylight from the gallery beyond. "She understands her duty. I have made sure of that."

"Leave us, Margaret," my father snapped. His eyes were straying again, out the window and across the sodden meadows beneath the castle keep. My aunt gave a loud *tut*. She swooped out of the room in a whoosh of black skirts and tapping cane.

Once she had gone and the door was shut, my father seemed to notice the shaking of my legs. He sat me down on the window seat and took my hand.

"Rosebud," he said quietly, using his private name for me. "Your mother would have been so proud of you."

The lady Rose, my mother, died when I was just four, and my recollection of her was no more than the scent of the rose petals that she used to dry and bring into my nursery to make it smell sweet. I had no memory of her beyond the narrow, mournful face with dark eyes in the portrait above our heads. But I did have a great sense of loss, a loss that my quicksilver, unreliable father could hardly fill. This mention of my mother, however, of whom he almost never spoke, dented the armour of my adulthood. I felt tears cloud my vision. This time I dipped my head so my father wouldn't see.

"You do understand, don't you?" There was an almost pleading note in his voice.

I thought that grown-ups never cried. Aunt Margaret had certainly told me that fine ladies always controlled themselves. But now I could have sworn that my father, even though he was fully grown and a baron as well, had a tear in his eye.

"Yes, Father," I said, tightening myself up inside just as Henny tightened the strings on my stays when she dressed me in fine clothes. "I know my duty."

Chapter 2

Dignified, *Elizabeth!*

6 NOVEMBER 1535

My father called for Henny, and she came in through the gallery door very quickly, just as if she'd had her ear to the door. She seemed curiously red around the eyes and was blinking hard.

"Take her and prepare her," my father said, then turned abruptly away. Henny took my hand. Although I really was too old to need to hold hands, there was something comforting about her rough grip today.

We made our curtseys, although my father seemed barely to notice, and Henny took me back along the gallery and away to our own rooms. The floors below were full of the sound of scuffing boots and laughter. Clearly, there were visitors downstairs in the belly of the house. I could hear our own servants talking, but there were also the loud voices of strange men. I turned to Henny to ask her who they were. But even I could tell, from the sight of her set face, that this was not a good time for questions.

Back in our chamber, Henny showed me a marvel—a new dress. On a normal dull day, I would have given all the hair of my head for a dress like this. But it just seemed part of the morning's general strangeness. Bewildered, I touched the stiff gold tissue of the overskirt and the sequins on the bodice with tentative fingers. "Yes, it is for you," said Henny, when she saw what I was doing, "and yes, you are going to wear it today." Henny washed my face in cold water, put me into a clean shift, shoved me forcefully into my farthingale, and popped the dress over my head. She did it up with an expression of fierce concentration.

"What are you doing?" I yelped, as she next untied my braid and began to pull a comb through the tangles of my hair.

"Today you are a bride," said Henny hoarsely, "and brides must wear their hair long, over their shoulders. When you are married, you will be old enough to put it up."

"Sit still and stop squirming!"

It was Aunt Margaret creeping up on us once again in her usual sinister fashion. I hardly heard her words. I was so used to her constant stream of instructions and complaints about my inability to sit still and my habit of running instead of walking that her voice washed over me like water, leaving nothing behind.

I don't think, however, that she intended me to hear what she had said to Henny one day when I was playing behind the tapestries hung on the walls of my bedchamber. She'd said that I was as skinny as a broomstick and like a witch's cat with my squinty green eyes. Her words got me thinking that I would quite like to own a magical cat myself, but on balance I think I would rather not have heard.

"Yes, do sit still for a while, Eliza," Henny said, as I wriggled to see what she had done to my hair in the old piece of polished silver we used to see our reflections.

"It's not Eliza. It's Mistress Elizabeth!" I whined as I often did. I could hear Henny *harrumph* softly as she wielded the ivory comb a final time. She resigned herself to it, came round in front of me, and brought her face down near my own.

"Now, *my lady*," she said, looking into my eyes. "You look just as grand as the Princess Elizabeth herself."

"Oh, nonsense!" came Aunt Margaret's caustic voice from behind us. "Is she good and ready? And don't mention the Princess Elizabeth. All the world knows her father the king has taken against her and sent her away from court."

"Yes, Mistress Margaret," Henny said, drawing back slowly and gently pinching my scowling cheek.

"Now, Elizabeth," Aunt Margaret said, as she took Henny's place before me.

Here we go, I thought. *I've heard all this before.*

She used her hand to spin my chin from side to side, inspecting every inch of me. She had a little frown on her face, just as usual, but for once I felt she was really looking at me. And when she spoke, it wasn't in her usual sing-song drone.

"Today your troth will be plighted to the Earl of Westmorland's son. He's a viscount, which means that one day you will be a viscountess, and when his father dies you will be a countess. That's second only to a duchess or a princess. I don't want any of your jokings or frolickings."

"No, Aunt Margaret."

"And no sullen silences or frowns either. You must be *dignified*, Elizabeth."

"Yes, Aunt Margaret. Is he here now?" I asked, nervousness as well as curiosity stirring inside me.

"Lord love us, no!"

I squirmed for a little longer under her critical inspection, until she decided to take pity on my ignorance. "Up in the Great Chamber, we will meet his servant, the man he has sent to stand in. You will take his hand, and the contract will be signed in front of the priest. But this is all legally binding, you know; you will be as good as man and wife."

She must have seen something of my confusion on my face. "You don't actually meet your husband face-to-face until you're older, my dear," she said in a more kindly tone. "You think you're all grown-up already, but you need to wait until your menses begin before you can live with him as a wife."

I nodded wisely, although I didn't really know what she meant. But there was no fooling my aunt Margaret. "Menses are certain pains that will come upon you, child, when you're old enough to have a child of your own," she said. I sensed that Henny and Aunt Margaret were looking at each other silently over the top of my head, and I didn't like the feeling of being excluded.

"What pains?" I asked, a little crossly.

"Never mind about that now," Aunt Margaret said, giving me a smart tap with her cane and shooing me out of my seat.

Chapter 3

The Westmorland Blackbird

6 NOVEMBER 1535

We returned to the Great Chamber to find an elderly man in black standing with my father in the place of honour by the fire—roaring for once with hefty logs. My father was holding the poker, as if he had been fiddling with the fire. It looked odd because I had often heard him claim that Camperdownes never felt the cold.

"Ah, my daughter Elizabeth!" he said in a hearty loud voice, as if he had not seen me for weeks.

Embarrassed, I found it impossible to look at him and scanned the room instead.

Around its edges there were now gathered many people well known to me, including my father's steward and servants from our household. I had many friends among the servants, like Mistress Cox the cook, who would let me steal a piece of pie from her echoing stone kitchen, and Susan the dairy-maid, who would give me a spoonful of cheese if I helped her stir the curds. Today, though, their familiar faces were lapped on all sides by strangers whom I'd never seen before.

Henny was whispering in my ear. "You see that gentleman, Sir Dudley?" she said, nodding at the figure in black. "Today you'll take his hand in place of that of your real husband. It's just a ceremony." The corners of my mouth drooped in chagrin. I had to reassure myself with the memory of my aunt's earlier words that it would still count as a proper legal betrothal.

"But he's so *old*!" I whispered back, perhaps more loudly than I'd realised, for a muffled sound in the background might have been a suppressed laugh from Aunt Margaret's maid Betsy. It occurred to me to wonder what my actual husband would be like.

Would he be an ancient old man as well? In all my daydreams, my future spouse had been dashing and young, like Sir Lancelot.

Fortunately, Sir Dudley himself came forward, twitching his head like a bird, and took my hand in a friendly way. Despite this, he looked intimidating, with the silver stitching on his doublet, his neat white beard, and his generally foreign air. I knew that Henny would be sure to say later he had what she called a "court smell," as if he ate different food and breathed different air from normal Derbyshire people. Although Sir Dudley had only travelled from his master the earl's house in Westmorland, I imagined that everybody at the king's court had his sleek, well-groomed look.

Sir Dudley took my hand and drew me aside from the rest, to a table close to the window. The table was covered with a dark red and green Turkish carpet, upon which lay several sparkling objects. Instantly, my attention was captured, for I love treasures of all kinds. There was a pile of fine moony pearls, a gorgeous ring, and a silver brooch in the shape of the letter "E." On the top of the "E" sat a curious bird with its beak open. I began to hope that the brooch, with my own initial, might possibly be a gift.

"Are these my birthday presents?" I asked with some hesitation, for I knew that it was wrong to want other people's things, to *covet* them as Aunt Margaret called it. According to her, I had an unduly *covetous nature* that I was supposed to try to keep in check.

"Well, yes, of course, as it's your birthday, they might be," Sir Dudley said. "But they are also betrothal presents from your future husband, the viscount." At this he knelt down and gestured invitingly to the glittering things, like one of the ancient eastern Magi bringing treasures to the Nativity.

"What, all of them?" I sensed that my eyes were open extra wide. I believe I was pulling an expression called "dumbstruck," like that of poor old Tub, the boy who'd been stricken speechless in Stoneton village as a punishment for stealing and whose words could never pop out of his endlessly open lips.

"Indeed. These pearls of Barbary are to add to the rope of pearls that belonged to your mother, the lady Rose," he explained. I felt a moment's annoyance that he, a stranger, could speak of my mother. "And this is a ring, a symbol of your husband's great love for you," he said, successfully distracting me by slipping it onto my finger. Of course, I was distressed to realise it was much too big. "And this brooch, with your own initial, is topped with the crest of your new family, the Westmorland blackbird." He then pointed out to me that the strangers in the room were each wearing a similar metal badge with the strange silver bird on it. One by one they pointed to their own silver birds and smiled encouragingly.

"This is your new family," he said, as he led me to a table where another man was scratching away with a quill upon a sheaf of parchment.

"And this," said my father, very softly in my ear, "is where you must sign to finalise the contract." He picked up the quill and put it in my hand. "Can you remember how to write your name?"

"Of course I can!" I replied, stung, and it was with a sense of injured pride that I laboriously signed E. *Camperdowne*. I added a flourish below my name.

With my dress and my ring, I felt ready to take my place as a countess. I began to imagine myself strolling through one of the royal palaces, nodding graciously to gentlemen even finer than Sir Dudley who bowed down at the sight of me. Surely the king himself would be glad to know me.

Replacing the pen, I tried to stand up extra straight, almost as if there were already a crown on my head. I could hear a murmur of pleasure from the people in the room behind me: Henny, Betsy, the Stewards, the Woods, Mr. Nutkin, Mistress Cox, and Susan of our household, and all the new strangers marked out by their blackbird badges. I even saw a thin smile on Aunt Margaret's lips, and she gave me a slight but distinct nod.

This was the first tottering step I took, I believe, on the path towards restoring the Camperdownes to their rightful place in the world.

I had no notion that it would take so many turns, both for good — and for ill.

Chapter 4

You'll Meet Your Husband!

1536

I was proud that I had played my part well. I knew I had excelled because my father told me so. We were sitting at the top table in the Great Hall while all the tenants and guests ate enormous slices of roast beef, and then (glorious moment) raised their cups to drink to my health. At that I bowed my thanks as if I were already a countess. After dispensing my stately nods to the left and right, I took a gulp of sack myself, but it was so sweet and strong, it made me feel a little sick. How could adults drink that stuff?

Within a few days, I had grown more used to the idea that I was betrothed and that no one but God could part me from my aristocratic husband. I longed for my menses to start, so that I could be a properly married lady and go to live in my husband's house.

"When will I leave here to go and live at Westmorland, Aunt Margaret?" I asked each and every morning. "When, when, when?"

"Oh, for the love of God!" she snapped back at me. "Anyone would think you disliked your home and family."

I pondered her words. The turrets at Stoneton were a little crumbly around the top, like a biscuit that you had carried in your pocket, and the gardens below were rather fuller of vegetables than pleasure grounds should really be. Yes, of course I loved this place, but it was so run-down and boring.

Probably once I was there at Westmorland, there'd be presents like those Sir Dudley had given me *every day*, and no longer would I have to attend the boring daily grind of lessons in writing or housekeeping. Probably I would wear a pink gown and a tall pointed hat with a veil floating from the top of it, like the ladies did at the court of Prince

Arthur. But within a week, our guests had departed, and life mysteriously seemed to have returned to its usual placid course. It was just as if Sir Dudley had never visited and my father had never nearly cried.

Sometimes I nearly cried myself, in the grey mornings, as I woke in my same old bed to rain outside and to a long boring day of the usual lessons and tasks. I thought longingly of the pearls, the ring, and the silver brooch, taken away from me and hidden safely in a closet so that I couldn't lose or break them. But as the weeks stretched on, I gradually returned my attention to my old doll, Sukey, to my whip, and to my little model knights. Although they were the same old toys, I did invent some new games.

Previously, the knights had been engaged in a lengthy war against the evil bodkins, whose fortress was the sewing box. But now they preferred to rescue Sukey from the dark and powerful forces occupying the clothes chest, uniting their puny strength to carry her along upon a palanquin fashioned from a velvet cushion.

Aunt Margaret was just as tiresome as before,

lecturing me on how I was far too old to play with Sukey now.

Along with my beloved Henny, I saw my aunt every single day. My father, on the other hand, came and went on visits as colourful but as short as the lives of the blowsy pink roses that blossomed around the pointed stone porch that led into our Great Hall. During the dreary stretches when he was away, I always told people the king was keeping him busy "at court." Really, though, I knew that often he was only visiting our outlying estates.

When my father was at home, my morning lessons were fun, exciting even. Sometimes he would stride in unexpectedly, dismissing Aunt Margaret. He would tell me about strange lands beyond the sea, lands from which our spices came and that were populated by men with one eye and one leg. Or sometimes he would show me his astrolabe. And now that I was betrothed, we would occasionally decipher books by putting English and Latin side by side, so that I could help my future husband with his legal affairs and his library.

But my aunt's lessons were a much more mundane affair, more often than not to do with the necessity of being a good Christian, giving alms to the poor, sitting up straight, and behaving correctly in company. If we did writing, I had to copy out A *maid should be seen and not heard*, and I was supposed to embroider the same words onto the cushion I had been working on for a good eighteen months. However hard I tried, I never got further than A *maid should* . . . I often completed it in different ways in my head, like A *maid should never touch a needle* or A *maid should kill dragons*.

After my betrothal, I felt even more impatient than usual with Aunt Margaret's attempts to teach me how to make cordials in our still room and cream cheeses in our dairy. She forced me to watch as again and again she and Henny turned out cordials in one, or squidgy white cheeses in the other.

"But, Aunt," I cried, "I'm going to be a countess very shortly. I shall have many, many women to do these jobs for me."

"And if you don't know how to do things properly

for yourself, Elizabeth, they will trick you and skimp you in their work," she rapped back at me, as I swizzled the wooden dipstick in the honeypot.

So we went steadily on through the twelve days of Christmas and through the deadest, coldest, greyest part of the Derbyshire year. The long evenings had the compensation of tales told by the fireside from long-ago times, of battles and ghosts and strange spirits of the hills. The stories were recounted to all the household servants gathered together in the Great Hall by our old men, blind Mr. Nutkin and ancient Mr. Steward, the father of the current Mr. Steward.

When the catkins came at last, though, my father came home, and this time he had genuinely been at court and had ridden all the way from London. We were gathered outside the porch to meet him, having expected him all day.

"News!" he said, panting, almost before he was off his horse. "In June the king is to travel on progress round the country. And he's coming to Derbyshire!"

Aunt Margaret had grabbed the horse's head, even though the stable boy was ready to do it. If I didn't know that her blood was cold, like a lizard's, I'd have said she was excited.

"Will he come here? Anthony! Will he come to Stoneton?"

"Not to Stoneton," said my father regretfully, jumping down from the saddle. He turned to pick me up round the waist and swing me up towards the sky. "But almost as good. He's staying with the Earl of Westmorland, in his fine new house, and we're all invited. You're going too, Eliza, to meet the king."

I whooped out loud as he whooshed me through the air. When he had set me down on the ground once more, he turned to instruct the stable boy. But then, over his shoulder, almost as an afterthought, he tossed out another piece of information.

And this was the one that really made my heart thud like the galloping hoofs of my father's horse.

"Of course, Eliza, you'll meet the earl's son. Your husband!"

Chapter 5

Westmorland House

JUNE 1536

I was sick with excitement. For several days after hearing the news, I could not eat my supper or drink my bedtime milk. Henny gave a squeeze to my skinny shoulders one night as I turned away my lips from the cup. "Child, child," she sighed. "How will you ever grow bonny and buxom if you can't eat and drink properly?"

I pondered her words later as I lay in the dark, and I remembered my aunt calling me a broomstick. It occurred to me for the first time that the viscount, my husband, might possibly find me unsatisfactory or disappointing. My excitement was dampened down by a thin little mist of dread.

At last, in the first week of June, more than six months after my proxy marriage, the fine day dawned when we were to set off in our wagon. It was painted on the outside with our family's pink rose. I knew that eventually I would grow queasy with its swaying motion, but I could not wait to climb aboard. Although I was wearing an old blue dress, I had seen Henny packing away the gold one in our trunk. I was inside the wagon, bouncing impatiently upon my velvet seat, long before the packhorses were even loaded with our boxes.

Out of the corner of my eye, I saw that Mistress Cox and Susan had come out into the stone courtyard to see us off, but I was too busy looking ahead and thinking about my life as a countess to acknowledge them. I'm sorry to say that I probably even neglected to respond when Mr. Nutkin and Mr. Steward called out, "God bless."

We travelled all day, stopping to eat pies and chicken at the house of one of my father's tenants. I had been there before, but the second stop we made for the horses to rest was at a strange house belonging to a tenant of the earl's. Carved into the fireplace of this farmer's house, I spotted the bird with its open beak, and I looked forward to wearing my own similar silver brooch. I knew Aunt Margaret had it safe in our luggage, because after some considerable nagging on my part, she had shown it to me last night.

For most of the long day's journey, Aunt Margaret made me sit up straight. In the afternoon, though, she nodded off to sleep, and in no time at all, I was poking my head out the side of the wagon to watch the woods passing by and trying to glimpse my father riding ahead of us on his horse.

At last, at dusk, we began to wind our way downhill through a forest, and the wagon paused. My father was calling. "Come out and stretch your legs," he urged. "We're nearly there, and you can see the house from here." I fairly sprang out the door and landed on the leafy trail with an ungainly thud.

As I straightened myself up, I saw between the trees the massive block of Westmorland House. Set in its broad valley, it looked more like a small town, with extensive gardens and outbuildings all around it, not crammed onto a hilltop like Stoneton. All the windows seemed to be open to take in the soft evening air. I could see figures walking about on the flat leads of the roof and many more in the courts and gardens below. To one side, a great red tent had been pitched, and even now men were tugging the ropes to erect another.

I must have given an involuntary gasp, for my father gave a little snort of amusement. I quickly snapped my mouth closed. But he could tell that I wanted to know what the tents were for, and he was in a mood to humour me. "They're erecting extra accommodation," he explained, "for all the people who have come with His Majesty and Queen Jane. The house, big though it is, isn't big enough."

I knew that the king had recently exchanged the old queen, Queen Anne Boleyn, for a new queen whose name was Jane. This was important News From Court, and I prided myself on being up-to-date. But I couldn't seem to speak and only just managed silently to nod my head. I was still busy looking at everything.

My father's hand closed on my shoulder, firmly

but also sternly. "One day," he said softly, "this will be your home. But you must never forget Stoneton. You will have to do whatever it may take to keep Stoneton standing proud. It's your duty."

I nodded my head vigorously, swallowing hard. My future home was bigger than I'd expected, and consequently I felt that I myself was a little smaller than usual. Would the king even notice me among all those people?

So it was almost reluctantly that I climbed back on board the wagon, and we clattered down the rolling hillside, through the gardens and into the courtyard.

Although I thought it would have been exciting to sleep in a tent, Aunt Margaret explained that the Camperdowne family was too important not to have a room in the house. We were allocated a chamber up a staircase off a courtyard. This turned out to be a little smaller and darker than my bedroom at Stoneton, although it was very richly furnished with silver candlesticks instead of pewter, and beer was brought up to us in a jug without our even having asked for it.

Everyone was pleased to have arrived. Even Aunt

Margaret failed to check under the bed for dust and instead told Betsy and Henny to open our trunks as quickly as possible so as to dress for the feast. As Betsy fastened the clasp of Aunt Margaret's amethyst necklace over her purple dress, I thought that my grey old aunt seemed transformed.

"You look like the fairy queen!" I said in wonder, and tried to stroke the amethysts. The chill that had fallen upon me earlier was quite blown away by the bustle of getting ready for the party. But she batted my hand away. "What about me — shall I wear my gold dress?" I asked as I tugged her skirt.

"Child!" Aunt Margaret said. "Of course you won't be going to the feast tonight. As soon as Henny has brought your bread-and-milk, you'll be tucked up into this snug bed, and I'll join you later to keep you company. And sleep deep!" she said, as she must have seen my face fall. "Rest well! Tomorrow you'll meet your husband, Elizabeth!"

Half an hour later, Henny had coaxed me to swallow some soggy and oversweet bread-and-milk, and then even told me my favourite story about Sir

Lancelot in the hope of sending me off to sleep. But I rebelliously kept my eyes open extra wide.

"Now then, Eliza!" she said, as I fidgeted about and kicked against the sheet. "Don't you want to hear how he defeats the monster?"

"It's Mistress Elizabeth," I said, rolling to turn away from her. In the end she gave up and simply left me alone, not unwillingly, I sensed, for I knew that she too wanted to explore the wonders of Westmorland.

And so did I. Tentatively, as if someone might have been listening, I sat up in bed, and then slipped my feet down to the floor. They met a soft sheepskin, something we didn't have at home. I wiggled my toes in it and revelled in the luxurious feeling it gave me. It was still summer twilight, and I could examine it quite easily without the need for a candle.

I pressed my ear to the door, trying to hear the sounds below. There was a low murmur of movement, voices, possibly distant music.

"Fiddlesticks! It's just not fair."

I spoke right out loud, as if to that imaginary listener. It seemed truly intolerable that I should have been left up here to moulder away by myself.

In a moment or two, I had lifted the cold iron latch (we had wooden ones at Stoneton) without making too much noise and was looking out at the narrow staircase that had brought us to our rooms.

I crept down, soundless in my bare feet, regretting that I was wearing my linen shift and not my gold satin dress. The shift itself was rather old and had shrunk in the laundry. I could almost hear Aunt Margaret's voice in my head, exclaiming at the foolishness and loss of dignity in going about improperly dressed.

At the bottom of the staircase was a cloister, open to the shadowy courtyard. The cloister was empty, but in the space beyond were torches and figures and sound: such a coming and going, with well-dressed ladies scurrying about, kissing each other, and emitting shrieks of laughter, and menservants carrying flaming torches.

Suddenly, from my left, came a group of men all dressed alike in green, half running, and each of them carrying what I guessed was a different type of musical instrument. I recognised a lute and a recorder, but the rest I had never seen before.

Once the musicians had scurried out of sight, though, a sudden hush fell over the whole courtyard. It was almost like the blowing out of a candle.

Everyone remaining stopped walking and sank to his or her knees. Every hat left its owner's head. A bulky, richly dressed figure was parading slowly through the throng. He was leading by the hand a tiny lady no less lavish in dress, both of them stepping with immense dignity. I could only see their silhouettes, in profile, except for where the torchlight gleamed on the satin and gold of their clothes. Surely this was the king and Queen Jane! I knew for certain, by the response of everybody about them, that these people were powerful, mysterious, and glamorous. They looked like angels from heaven or creatures from another world.

I almost cried with vexation. I wanted nothing more than to see the king and queen properly. But that would never happen while I was in my underwear.

Only once they had gone in the direction of the Great Hall did normal life start again.

"Watch out there, skulking in the dark!" called a voice. I looked along the cloister to my right to see a servant maid, bearing down upon me with an enormous bowl. It might have contained water or someone's ordure; I wasn't sure which. I also thought I had better not wait to find out. I whisked about and retreated to my staircase, hoping that the maid was too busy to investigate. With my heart still thudding from the shock of being shouted at, I crept back up.

Once at our own door, though, I simply couldn't face the bed to which I had been banished while everyone else was meeting the earl and having a magnificent time. Instead, I climbed up past our door and round several more twists and further doorways. The wall, which had been finely plastered, turned into plain brick, and the floor, which lower down had been swept clean, was scattered with dust and bird droppings. At the very top, I popped out through a little door onto the roof.

From this vantage point, I could see the whole house spread before me and many of its inhabitants rushing about their business. All the earl's friends and neighbours must have been in attendance for the king's visit. I had never seen so many people. Standing on my toes to peer over the brick battlements, I could see lights pricking out in the gardens and a glow inside the red fabric of the tents. I could hear a raucous buzz rising from the hall, where the guests must have been eating, and saw swarms of serving men, like ants, running with dishes across the courtyard. I believe I may have emitted a sigh of pleasure.

"Seen something, or someone, tasty?"

I whipped around. A languid young man was uncoiling himself from a kind of step in the roof, where he'd been sitting. He raised the goblet he held in his hand and said, "I drink to you, my lady!"

I was pleased that he had recognised a future countess, even in her nightgown. I stood a little straighter and raised my chin as Aunt Margaret would have advised. At the same time, though, I had a sneaking suspicion that he was not taking me as seriously as I would have liked.

The gentleman — for surely he was a gentleman, not a servant — wasn't old, like my father or Sir Dudley, but he wasn't as young as me either. (Later I was to discover that he was eighteen.) He had a dashing curve of dark hair across his forehead, a shirt that was undone all down the middle, and—curiously—no shoes. He'd been sitting on his doublet, and I knew that Henny would have castigated me for crushing such a fine satin garment.

He didn't speak like a servant, yet he wasn't properly dressed. He was up here all alone, yet he had his goblet and more wine beside him as if for a party. Although I tried to hide it by looking prim, I could also tell that he was more interesting than anyone I'd ever met.

"Thank you, sir," I replied. Then, after a pause and some inward debate, I dropped the curtsey I felt sure my aunt would have advised.

This seemed to please him enormously. "Ah, Skinny Ribs has all the courtly arts!" He laughed. "Come and have a swig of wine." Now I was sure that he was joking. Cross at being called Skinny Ribs, I backed up against the parapet and bristled like a cat.

"No, thank you," I said. "I shall shortly be going to dine with the earl."

"Oh, so you know the Earl of Westmorland, do you?" he asked nonchalantly, as if he knew all the earls in the world and didn't think much of them.

"Indeed I do," I said, drawing myself up tall, "and one day I shall be the Countess of Westmorland myself. I am already my father's heiress, though, and our family of Camperdowne is even older than that of the Westmorlands." I expected another toast, at least a bow of the head, but instead the young man doubled up with a loud guffaw.

"Well," he said, "what a little tomcat! Indeed, *my lady*, you should aim higher in marriage than the f-family of Westmorland." Curiously, he seemed to have trouble with the word "family" and combined it with a hiccup. "Why not aim as high as the lady Anne Boleyn did, for example? Why not aim for the hand of the king himself?"

"Well, he is married to Queen Jane now," I said tartly, ducking backwards. "But of course," I went on boldly, "I hope shortly to make the king's acquaintance. Once I am a countess, that is. I'm sure he will be pleased to meet me."

At this the young man doubled over as if in pain, but then let out what was surely a hoot of laughter. This enraged me, and for a second I was close to flying at him. I even stamped my foot and slightly stubbed my bare toe upon the brick battlement. But then a thought must have occurred to him that seemed to check his hilarity, for he looked all around, as if to confirm that there was no one else on the roof with us.

"Of course we mustn't mention," he said in a stage whisper, "the possibility of anyone taking Queen Jane's place. His Majesty is very much in love."

Heaving himself up, he came over and stood close to me, still smiling and smelling quite sharply of stale sweat. I could now see spots of wine and other stains on his linen, tainting my first impression of careless glamour.

At once I felt that the young man, initially so intriguing, contained a hint of menace. "Good night, my master, and God bless your sleep," I gabbled, as I had been taught, curtseyed again, and backed down the staircase.

"Good night, my lady tomcat!" were his mocking words.

And that, as I would later learn, was my first conversation with the man who was to be my husband.

Chapter 6

Disgrace

JUNE 1536

The row was terrible the next day when it all came out and Aunt Margaret discovered where I had been and what I had done.

The morning had started well enough. We had all progressed to the earl's chamber, dressed in our best. At my father's nudge in my back, I stepped forward, knelt low, and kissed the grand old earl's hand. My father did not really look like a baron, but this old earl certainly looked like my idea of an earl. His commanding figure, with craggy nose and chin, was on the right scale for the room. It was twice the size of ours at Stoneton, and the earl sat on a red velvet chair beneath a red velvet canopy. But I was hardly able to enjoy a good stare at him, for after my curtsey, I dared not look up at the formidable face. Even then I felt a sneaking feeling of shame at having claimed his acquaintance to the stranger on the roof last night.

Next there was a long pause, and my father cocked his head in a way that I knew indicated the beginnings of impatience.

The earl cleared his throat. No one seemed to have the audacity to make conversation. I very much wanted, but did not dare, to ask which of the crowd of men present was my husband. Aunt Margaret beside me was very softly clicking her tongue. This sound forced me to swallow a grin. For once, my aunt wasn't able to boss her way out of the situation.

Finally, a servant stepped forward into the room, and I sensed Aunt Margaret shift her weight with relief. Clearly, the hitch in the proceedings, whatever it was, would now be untangled, and we could go on with the meeting.

But the young man paused, with a show of

reluctance. The earl had to gesture sharply at him to speak.

"As the viscount spent last night with the Mistress Elizabeth, he feels she will accept his apologies for being too unwell to see her in person this morning."

There was an extremely long silence, during which I felt rather than saw the disdainful gaze of the earl turn towards me, and then penetrate right through me. I felt Aunt Margaret stiffen by my side, and my father too turned his foxy stare upon me. No one seemed to know what to do. Eventually, my father and aunt took me by each arm and hurried me from the room.

Back in our chamber, my father looked at me hard. "Leave us, Henny!" he barked out grimly. His eyes never left me while she slipped silently out of the room. "What have you got to say?" he asked, standing very still.

My heart sank down to my slippers. Hanging my head and mumbling my words, I had to reveal that I had indeed met an unknown young man last night when I should have been in bed. "The Lord have mercy upon us!" said Aunt Margaret almost inaudibly. "She is her headstrong uncle all over again."

My father looked at me for a moment, before turning and marching out without speaking.

I guessed what would happen next, and I was right. Aunt Margaret laid her cane across my buttocks in a manner put aside since I was eight or nine.

"Bringing — shame — and — disgrace — upon our — family!" she grunted through clenched teeth, matching each word to a stroke.

"But what have I done?" I howled in genuine misery and despair, trying unsuccessfully to writhe and twist my body away from her reach. "I only went up the stairs. I only wanted to see the party."

"You have embarrassed your father, you have acted like a harlot, and you have made *me* look like I have no control over you," she snarled, as she raised the cane again.

Despite my protestations, I knew that I had done wrong. My father and aunt were clearly sickened by my behaviour, but I don't believe that they were as sickened as I was. I almost swayed with shame as I recalled my boasting and the fact that my husband had seen me in my shift and called me Tomcat. I did not dare to ask what my husband had himself been doing up on the roof, but I assumed that a viscount in his own father's house could go wherever he liked and drink as much wine as he wanted.

Once my beating was over, I heard my father speaking sharply in the outer room of our apartment to some emissary from the earl, saying that he would not tolerate the public insult given to his sister and his daughter in front of all those people. And so we left Westmorland House without my having met the king and Queen Jane after all. We departed for Stoneton that same evening in confusion and dismay, missing the week of feasting and hunting that had been planned.

Our own journey home passed in stiff silence, so different to the holiday air of our arrival. I dared not mention it to my father and my aunt, as I was in such trouble, but I longed to see the bold young man of the rooftop once again. To myself I had half explained away his odd manner. Perhaps he had climbed up on the rooftop because he could read the stars, like a magician. Or perhaps he had been resting up there after a flight on his flying carpet. Maybe, in due course, he would take me with him.

At home life returned to normal, and no one said anything about my marriage. It seemed that what I had done was too bad even to talk about.

Weeks rolled by, and with them the haymaking and the blackberry seasons. But I could not enjoy them as usual. No one mentioned Westmorland, and slowly I began to fear that I would never go to live there with my husband after all. Perhaps people were already saying behind my back that I had been rejected.

"Oh, Sukey!" I would sigh each day, as I took her from the toy chest. "I have a bold, saucy nature. Aunt Margaret says so. You're so quiet and as good as gold. I wish I were more like you." And yet I longed, more than anything, to believe that I was still going to be a countess.

At night I would often cry myself to sleep, and even in the sunny mornings there seemed very little reason to get out of bed. I moped about indoors, unable to settle to any task. I could see that Henny was worried about me, but I didn't know how to set her mind at rest. How could I?

I confided only in Sukey.

"Stoneton might crumble and fall into ruin because of what I did," I told her sternly. "Henny might have to go and ask for alms from the parish." A terrible thought struck me. "Or she might even starve." Blinking hard and throwing my doll down onto the floor, I cursed the silent Sukey for her lack of sympathy.

One warm evening some weeks later, my father called me to the garden. He sat on the stone seat with a letter on his lap.

"Eliza," he said kindly, almost as if I weren't in disgrace. "You must set your hopes aside of being the Countess of Westmorland. I call down God's vengeance upon that blackguard family."

"Oh, Father, I am very sorry," I said, throwing my arms around him. "I know I shouldn't have done it." A great racking rainstorm of tears overtook me, and I gave way to it almost gratefully. I had tried so hard for so long not to let my feelings show.

My father seemed a little lost for words and gave me an awkward pat on the back.

"Oh, Rosebud, you were very rash and foolish,

but we will teach you to be more ladylike in time," he said. "Now listen to me carefully."

He took a deep breath and put his finger under my chin. I wanted to know what he was going to say so much that I had to stop sobbing. "Little Rosebud, this matter of your marriage is a setback, but it isn't the end of our hopes. It turns out that the Earl of Westmorland was deceived in his son. The viscount, whom you met, is a bad young man. He drinks too much and carouses, and, it turns out, he was not free to marry you."

I pondered the matter, but I couldn't work it out.

"He already had a wife. At least I will say this for the old earl — he feels himself to be deeply shamed as well. He has a daughter-in-law of whom he cannot be proud, and he is gnashing his teeth. The lady his son has secretly married is a chambermaid at an inn, I believe, and now she is demanding a high fee to dissolve the union. Despite the secrecy, I understand that it was all done quite formally with a contract."

"Is that how King Henry got rid of Queen Anne?" I asked. "Did he pay her to go away so he could marry Queen Jane?"

I was thinking that perhaps my husband would likewise need to manage matters so that our own marriage would be valid after all.

"Eliza!" my father said sternly. "It's dangerous to speak of the old queen now. She had her head cut off for witchcraft and treason. You must never, ever make the same mistake. Thunder rolls around the throne."

"Will I have my head cut off for climbing up onto the roof?"

Now he even laughed. It was a sound I had almost forgotten, for I had not heard it for many weeks. "Rosebud, Rosebud," he said. "Listen to me. The important thing to realise is that you are *not* married to the Earl of Westmorland's son."

Only then, I think, did I truly begin to believe it. A worm of disappointment uncurled inside me, a malign sensation reaching up from my stomach and down my arms to my fingers. I crushed them into fists to brace myself.

"We were tricked, and the earl himself was tricked by his evil and lascivious son. But you are not ready for marriage either. Your behaviour at

Westmorland House has shown that you are not learning everything that you ought to here, all alone, at Stoneton. You will be going away shortly, to live with other people in the south. You are not going to be a countess. Instead, you are going to school."

Chapter 7

Headstrong Ways

1536

I stared at him, unable to take it in. I was to be sent away from Stoneton — to school? Surely that was impossible!

"Yes, I know," my father said, as my mouth opened and shut silently, like a fish. It was so quiet I could almost hear the dew falling around us on the grass.

"I know you want jewels," he continued, "and servants and *not* to do your lessons. I know all that." He took my two hands and gave them a squeeze, and smiled, a little sadly. "I wanted all those things too. But they don't just fall into your lap. And I hope that once you are away from your home, you might appreciate it more."

At that he rose and folded up his letter and gave me a little shove to go back indoors. The garden was growing dusky. "Bedtime!" he said, as if I were still just a baby.

Back in my bedchamber, I found that Henny knew all about it. "Your father and your aunt have decided that you are going to live with a relation of yours," she told me, "the Duchess of Northumberland."

As so often with Henny, she was folding my clothes as she talked. There was something comforting about her slow, repetitive movements. I sank onto my bed to listen.

"She is a very old lady, far too old for anyone to remember exactly when she was born. It must have been, I don't know, before the ending of the Wars of the Roses. She is admired and respected, I think, in the county of Hertfordshire, and she has so many children and grandchildren that her house is a kind of school. She employs teachers there for all her children's children."

At the word "teachers," I sucked in my breath and opened my mouth to complain. But Henny quickly went on.

"Lots of the girls there will be your relations, Eliza, and you will soon settle in and learn to love them."

"But, Henny," I asked desperately, "who will look after me? What will it be like?"

"Child!" Henny laughed and turned to dump a great pile of sheets into my arms. "I don't know. I've never been out of Derbyshire myself." Then she must have spotted my miserable face, and she softened her tone. "But you're my own little flaming firebrand, aren't you?" she said. "You can look after yourself! Now put these in the linen press, my love, and then get into bed."

Of course I knew that I would hate it. How could I go from being singular, special, and unique, the heiress to a noble family, to being just one more among the duchess's grandchildren and their cousins? I despised my father and aunt, and Henny too, for their lack of understanding, and I screamed and railed for many days before I finally and sullenly gave in and accepted that I had no power of refusal.

I could see that my aunt Margaret was tired almost to distraction by my dramatic carryings-on.

"Now, child," she said one day as we sat at our needlework in the Great Chamber, "there are many benefits to your going to the duchess's household. You will see how a great establishment works and how people behave in good society."

Instead of responding to her, I feinted at an imaginary enemy with my dagger (or spindle).

"Listen to me, Elizabeth!" she tried again. "You will learn polished manners and make good friends to help you in the future."

The hank of thread suddenly detached itself from my spindle and fell to the floor in a mess. With a loud sigh, I also hurled down the spindle itself.

Aunt Margaret's uncanny ability to be in two places at the same time came into play once again, and a harsh hand unexpectedly slapped the back of my head and made me yelp. "Now pick up that thread and sort it out," she said. "The most important lesson that you'll learn from the duchess is that you are not the centre of God's world. You need to lose those headstrong ways."

So it was that a few months later, after my thirteenth birthday, Henny and I were once again setting out on a journey. But this time we would be travelling much farther, into an entirely new part of England. And this time there was nothing to look forward to at the other end.

There was sourness in my final parting with my aunt and father, and I turned my face away and refused to answer when they tried to kiss me goodbye. I climbed in the wagon as fast as I could, just as I had when we had gone to Westmorland. But this time I did so because I wanted to crouch down on the floor and hide my face in the velvet seat. I no longer wanted to see my much-loved Stoneton, swathed now in autumn mist, a place that evidently I was no longer considered good enough to inhabit. And I had no intention of meeting the eyes of the father who had sent me away.

Worst of all, I could tell that Henny was disappointed in me. As our litter lurched into queasy motion, I could see that she regretted my refusal to say goodbye properly to those who had loved and looked after me for my whole life.

Only ten minutes later, when tears began silently to trickle down my face, did she hold out her hand to pass me something. Something soft. It was Sukey. The poor ragged old doll was a pitiful sight, but dear Henny had brought her along to try to cheer me up.

"Oh, Henny!" I choked. Clutching Sukey to my chest, I turned to Henny and pressed my teary face into my nurse's lap. "My mother would not have sent me away."

"Hush, hush, Eliza," Henny said. "Your father and aunt do love you, you know," she murmured into my ear. I lay there, while she stroked my hair for many hours as we travelled south.

During this journey we made together, she told me things that I will remember and hold dear for the rest of my life. She told me that my father and aunt were only acting for the best. She reassured me that they had been as hurt as I had by the failure of my marriage with the Earl of Westmorland's son, and that they wanted to find me a rich, powerful husband, to whom I would bear many children and live with in great comfort. To meet such a man, who was probably to be found at court, I needed to learn the art of pleasing, to be able to meet strangers with ease, and to live pleasantly with other people. There was no other way for people like my father and my aunt and me. We had to do our duty so that other folk, like Henny herself, would have somewhere like Stoneton, a safe place in which to live. And Henny herself told me that she was grateful and proud of me.

"Eliza, little Eliza!" she said. "I do love you as if you were my own girl, and it will break my heart to leave you in the south and travel back to Stoneton without you."

I learned later that Henny should not have said these things, and that generally it is wrong and against the order of things decreed by God and nature for a servant to speak in such a way. But at Stoneton matters were arranged differently. At Stoneton we all trusted each other, and although I have no brothers or sisters, I felt that everyone there was part of my family. Only in the big wide world beyond Stoneton's walls was I to learn that masters and servants sometimes hate and fear each other.

That night we slept in an inn, and I was so tired after my tears and our travel that I slept like a carved stone sleeper on a tomb in a church.

In the days that followed, we began to pass through towns larger than I had ever seen before, and rich tawny fields with fat brown cattle rather than sheep. We encountered creaking carts piled high with hay, and occasionally a great flock of geese being driven to market and completely blocking the road. Our wagon, with its coronet and the Camperdowne pink rose painted on its side, always let people know that we were gentlefolk, and the other traffic had to get out of our way. If there was any delay, our footman let loose with a volley of curses.

Once, a masterless man with a bristly face and ragged clothes reached up to our vehicle and banged on its side, shouting out that he wanted "Alms, for God's sake, some alms." But our footman leapt down with his stick to clear the vagrant away. Another time, outside an inn, a woman carrying a rolled-up quilt came over and showed me the wonderful coloured ribbons she had wrapped up inside it. But when Henny noticed, she spoke with uncharacteristic sharpness.

"We will save our money, thank you, madam!"

On the fifth day of travel, my eyes and ears felt sated with new sights and sounds, and Henny told me we were now in the county of Hertfordshire. We passed through a paling into a park of tall trees, broad enormous oaks in their autumn plumage of bronze, quite unlike the rather scraggy trees of Stoneton.

In the middle of this park was set a garden, with beds of lavender and hedges of box, a fountain and a great cage full of singing birds. And in the middle of the garden was something I'd never seen: a house built out of oak. It was called Trumpton Hall. My new home.

Part Two

At Trumpton Hall

Chapter 8

Welcome to Trumpton Hall!

1537
ELIZABETH IS THIRTEEN . . .

Henny and I climbed out of our litter, and a great number of maidservants and menservants seemed to materialise from behind the neatly clipped hedges to take our boxes and to show us to a room with a bowl of water and a polished mirror before meeting the duchess.

The house was snug and pleasantly scented inside. It had timber floors that moved a little as you walked and groaned as does — I imagine — the inside of a ship.

After we had washed and taken a drink, and Henny had knelt before me to straighten my dress, the oldest and sternest of the maids came to fetch us. The maid led us — me in front, Henny following — up a wide staircase. The light was red and blue from the coloured glass in the small panes of the windows. I could not help caressing the tail of a finely carved wooden leopard standing upon the turning of the bannisters. He was elegant and aloof, but extremely beautiful too. As I looked around, unwilling to leave him behind, I saw Henny give me an encouraging smile, and I almost smiled back.

We came out into the Great Chamber at the top of the stairs, which was filled with a rainbow of light from more stained glass. Painted upon its plaster walls were a wonderful unicorn in a forest and a walrus in an ocean.

But the unicorn and the walrus weren't the strangest creatures in that room. It was full of a noisy, chattering crowd of creatures I had never encountered before.

They were other girls.

I later learned that there were eight of them, but at first sight there seemed like many more, both big and small, talking with each other and running about. First one, then another, noticed me, and they all fell silent and stared. Henny whispered to me to curtsey and say my name. But first one of them, and then another, started to giggle.

"She's brought her Nursey!" said one of the girls.

"Nursey, Nursey!" called another. "Wipe my nosey, Nursey!"

"And, Nursey, I've hurt my finger!" shouted another.

"And, Nursey, be quick, I need the poo!" yelled a fourth over the growing sound of laughing and jeering. All the rest of them whooped and clapped. For a moment I wished the floor would open and swallow me. Through the hand she had on my shoulder, though, I could feel Henny stiffen, and on her behalf I found my courage.

"Do not be so rude to my tiring woman!" I snapped out, copying my father's most commanding voice.

"Oh, the little madam has a *tiring woman*, has she?" cooed one of the biggest girls, who came forward, hands upon her hips and swinging her skirt. She had a heavy jaw, but with her big eyes, she was utterly beautiful. "She's also got the carroty hair of the bastard daughter of the old Queen Anne. Are you illegitimate too, like her, *my lady Carrot Top*?"

I began to shake with rage. "I am far too well born to consort with the likes of you, you . . . cow!"

The word seemed both offensive and somehow accurate. Her eyes were so large and liquid, and her face so broad, even though she seemed to brim over with a luscious, milky beauty.

Indeed, I scored something of a point. One of the girls from the back let out a low "*Moooo!*"

The big girl turned angrily towards the miscreant, and I took the opportunity to replant the soles of my feet on the floor, glance at Henny, and take a deep breath to prepare for the next round.

There was to be no more sparring or teasing, however, because now the inner door flew open. Out came more maids. All the girls instantly turned to face the doorway and fell into a deep curtsey. The big, beautiful girl's demeanour had completely changed. No longer saucy and bossy, she was almost on the floor in the most graceful and submissive obeisance I had ever seen.

I was still so confused and hurt, though, that I failed to bob down, and when the Duchess of Northumberland came in, I was the only one left standing, staring like an awkward lonely stork. Only at Henny's urgent whisper did I clumsily sink to my knees.

"Elizabeth Camperdowne!"

The old duchess—white-haired but spritely, leaning on a long white stick—called out my name in a clipped voice, somehow making it sound strange rather than familiar. "Welcome to Trumpton Hall!"

At that moment, I felt I would rather be anywhere else in the world.

Chapter 9

Cousins

1537

How hard I wept when Henny had to leave the next morning. I clung to her arms so that she gently had to prise my fingers free. Once my father's wagon had departed through the woods and I could no longer see it, I felt that I might creep off and die somewhere by myself, like a very old dog. But there was nowhere I could go to be alone. Everywhere I went there were faces: cruel faces, yes, and one or two kindly ones as well. But all were nosy, their mouths asking constant questions.

It took me a long time to get straight all my relations at Trumpton Hall. The old duchess was rarely seen by the maidens, as we were called. If one of us heard her long white stick tapping along the passage as she came towards our chamber, there would be a sharp hiss of "The duchess!" Dice would be hidden, beds would be covered up, books snapped shut, and caps clapped back onto heads.

The eight other young ladies in the household were there, like me, to learn a little polish. We all slept together in the big attic room called "the maidens' chamber." From the duchess, who was grandmother to three of the girls, we would hear lengthy discourses on genealogy and the manner in which all of our families interlinked. Thus I learned that I was related to Katherine Howard, the boldest and buxomest among us, who had been so cruel to me upon my arrival. I also learned that there were many more families in England than I had thought.

"So you two are cousins!" said the duchess to us, her oldest and her newest students. She was concluding an explanation of a long parchment scroll with all the names of her relatives written in coloured ink and their coats of arms painted below them.

"Cousins!" Katherine exclaimed. "But I have never heard of the family of . . . what is it? Camden?"

"It's Camperdowne!" I cried out, dismayed. "The oldest family in Derbyshire!" And I stabbed with my finger at the pink rose beneath my father's name on the scroll.

"I cry you mercy," she said. "There are so many families nearer the king whose names we have had to memorise."

I turned to the duchess, expecting her to chastise her granddaughter for her rudeness, but a little smile flickered across her dry old face, almost as if she were amused by her star pupil's put-down.

The other girls had also looked to the duchess for a cue. They now turned towards me as if controlled by one mind, and each of them scorched me with a pursed, fake-looking smile of her own.

I looked down at my hands and sincerely swore to myself that one day I, too, would have a phalanx of ladies-in-waiting all of my own, who would smile like sour lemons at my enemies and make them feel as uncomfortable as I was feeling now.

But it wasn't all bad, even though I was reluctant

to admit it in the letters I wrote home to my family at Stoneton. From our dancing master, Monsieur Bleu, we learned the galliard, the deep court curtsey, and the best way to run in slippers while gracefully trailing a gauzy scarf. We learned that we should skip towards a gentleman as if we couldn't wait to meet him, at the same time divesting ourselves of a glove or a kerchief, garments that he would consider decorative but unnecessary.

We all learned to sing, although Anne Sweet, the youngest of us all, was the only one with a truly sweet voice. A little Italian was required, along with some light mathematics. All the girls were hoping to live at court some day, and we were told that many of the king's gentlemen there liked to dabble in astrology and science. We should be able to listen intelligently to their explanations of their discoveries.

"You were so quick!" said Anne Sweet to me one morning after we had taken our turn with the astrolabe and passed it on to our classmates. "How did you know how to use it? You must have done it before!"

Then I told her that my mother had died without having provided me with any brothers, and that my father had therefore taught me things that the other girls had no need to know. "I am the future of my family," I told her. "There's only me to carry on the line."

"Oh, Eliza!" said Anne. "You're so brave!" To my annoyance, the old, shortened version of my name seemed to have followed me here to Trumpton Hall. But Anne's chubby lips had fallen open into such a heartfelt "oh" of sympathy that I could not bring myself to tell her to call me "Elizabeth." Her very admiration made me sit up straighter in my chair.

But I was far behind Anne and the rest when it came to the lessons in beauty that we would take from the duchess's old waiting woman. "You've never used face powder?" Anne squealed, when I first confessed this. "What was your mother thinking of?"

Then the penny dropped as she remembered what I'd told her. Her cheeks turned crimson, and her mouth fell open once again. "Oh! Eliza! Forgive me!"

Full of apologies, she bustled me off to the dressing table in the corner of the maidens' chamber and sat me down amid the pots and jars.

"This is what you need to make your skin milky white," she said, dabbing at my cheeks with the white furry paw of a rabbit dipped in what looked like face powder. "Well, it's only fine white bread flour," she said in a rush, as if honesty compelled her to admit it, "but face powder does look like this. And here"— she handed me a cockle shell, in which nestled a sticky blob of red —"is cochineal. It's for the lips."

Using a finger, I carefully coated my mouth, pouting this way and that.

"Ooh, how adorable!" It was Katherine, coming into the room behind us and strolling over to watch, hands on her hips as usual. "The little girls are playing at being fine court ladies."

This made me whistle out a *harrumph*, and I gave her a hostile glare. But I could see that Katherine was interested in the tools and tinctures on the table. Perhaps the art of makeup was a skill worth acquiring after all. Annoyingly, Katherine was so pretty that I couldn't help admiring her a little. I could also tell, through Anne's delighted wriggles, that she, too, was basking in the attention of the queen of Trumpton Hall.

"Don't ask what this red stuff's made of," Katherine said, picking up the cockle shell in a majestic manner and applying a little to her own top lip. It had a deep curved shape to it that looked splendid picked out in red. "It's better not to know."

But this I could not bear.

"Katherine!" I cried. "Oh, do tell. I can't stand a mystery."

She knelt down beside me and put her face close to my own. "Well," she said slowly, "you did ask. I won't be held responsible. But my mother told me that it's made of the bodies of rare beetles, crushed up."

The thought almost made me gag. Shrieking, I wiped the red from my mouth as quickly as I could with a napkin. I felt physically sick.

"What are you laughing at, Anne?" I cried. "Beetles! That's disgusting!"

"But, Eliza," said Anne, "it's so funny. You look

exactly like my baby brother when he's been caught eating jam without bread. There's red all over your face."

Eventually, infected by their laughter, my own lips first wobbled, then giggled all by themselves. "Well, then," I said. "When I'm a fine court lady, I'm just going to use jam to stain my lips, not horrible beetles."

At this Katherine stood up and tousled my hair. "That's an excellent thought," she said. "Tasty lips. They'd be nice to kiss too."

I reminded myself that I disliked Katherine, but I could tell from Anne's proud nod that having had her spend time with us at the dressing table was something of a privilege.

"See you later, Carrot Top," Katherine said, as she swept swiftly out of the room.

Once again I inwardly gnashed my teeth. I was fed up with gibes about my red hair, even though Anne always came to my defence and did so now.

"The king himself has red hair," she said to me, "so I don't know how people can say that red hair means you've been taken by the devil. If it were true, it would apply to the king as well!"

"And, anyway," I said grumpily, trying to put my hair straight where Katherine had messed with it, "I would not care if the devil came to get me. I would kick him in the shins."

I was grateful to Anne and did my best to be proud of my distinctive hair. It had seemed so fine and bold back at Stoneton, but now I was in the south, I had secretly begun to wish that I had dark curling hair, blue eyes, full lips, and, above all, a bonny buxom chest like Katherine's.

Anne also showed me the art of positioning the hoods we had to wear so that a gentleman would notice the vulnerable nape of our necks from behind. "If we expose our necks," Anne said, "old Abigail says that a gentleman will feel a strange compulsion to place his hand upon them, and that will give him a pleasant feeling of great power."

Her message was reinforced by Abigail, the duchess's elderly waiting woman, in person. In her lessons, she constantly thrust an unfortunate analogy down our throats with respect to our deportment. "Imagine the trembling deer in the woods!" she would beg us in her quavering voice, gesturing with her hands like a dying swan. "Tremble, tremble, and offer up your neck as if it could be snapped in an instant!"

Her unfortunate imagery and choice of words made us call Abigail "Old Trembles" among ourselves. But the graceful extension of our necks for the wearing of future coronets was a lesson we all enjoyed.

The best lessons of all, and the ones in which I first began to enjoy myself at Trumpton Hall, were our studies in writing and in the notation of music. Master Manham, our teacher for these subjects, wasn't old like Monsieur Bleu, but young and very well shaped indeed. All of us considered ourselves to be in love with him. At night in the maidens' chamber, when we were all in bed but not yet asleep, one of us would describe how nicely his calves filled his stockings. Or another would claim he had slipped her an extra plum under the table during dinner.

At first I would lie quietly on my little low bed and merely listen to the competitive outpourings about Master Manham. As time went on, though, I found that meek Anne Sweet's questions about my family and my home helped to melt away my reserve. And I found that I wanted the other girls to know that I had some personal experience with men and with love. After all, I had been betrothed.

I told Anne the whole story one afternoon when we were by ourselves, and in the evening she begged me to tell the story again to the maidens' chamber in general.

"What?" gasped Juliana. "You are betrothed already? You are very young for that, Eliza."

"Yes, indeed," I said casually. "I was all set to become a countess. It was nothing to me really, as the title of Westmorland is much less ancient than my own family's."

But Katherine was too sharp to let it rest at that. "You said you *were* betrothed," she pointed out. "But you didn't say you *are* betrothed. What happened? Was it broken off?"

"Yes, there was . . . an administrative hitch."

"He wanted a wife with a proper bosom, more like," snorted Alice, another girl who was in cahoots with Katherine. She even managed to roll over in her bed in a dismissive manner.

"Actually, Eliza was too good for him." It was Anne's clear piping voice. "And her father realised it. She will hold out for a better offer than a viscount."

She had the attention of the room.

"Eliza told me this in confidence," Anne went on, "and I know she is too modest to tell you all. But I feel you should know the truth."

I blessed my loyal Anne and silently blew her a kiss through the dark. I wished I had never mentioned the business of the Earl of Westmorland's son, which did me no credit at all, but dear Anne had painted it in the best possible colours.

I also promised myself to speak less of my family and its antiquity, and to think a little more of trying to make my cousins like me. For sometimes, as I lay alone and full of pride, I felt jealous of their pillow fights and their discussions of which stable boy was the most handsome.

Of course I would do my duty at court, when the time came. That would involve winning the richest and highest-ranking husband, and making him fall in love with me rather than with Alice or Juliana. But here at Trumpton, I thought it could not hurt me, sometimes, to be a bit more like them.

Chapter 10

In the Maidens' Chamber

1537

But then came my great setback. The heat of the afternoon one Sunday forced us to come indoors from the garden. Everyone was arguing over which room downstairs would be coolest for our Bible reading. As they tried out one room and then another, I ran upstairs to use the privy in the tiny closet off our maidens' chamber.

Before I had finished, though, I heard Katherine and one of the other girls entering the room, clearly thinking themselves to be alone. I dared not step forth once they had begun to converse.

"Little Carrot Top has left her things in a mess again, I see!" called out Juliana, and I had a horrible feeling that she might have been fiddling or tweaking with my bedcovers or my underclothes. I must admit I had left them in some disorder.

"Quite! She thinks that she's far too good for the rest of us," came Katherine's languid reply. "What a lazy little snob! She thinks she's so grand that she doesn't need to keep her stuff tidy, but the funniest thing is that she doesn't realise what a comical rustic she sounds like, with her north country accent."

My hands clenched themselves into fists, and the pit of my belly dropped down towards the floor. While I had warmed to Anne Sweet and even sometimes to Alice, I wasn't sure what to think about Katherine, our natural leader. I hid my feelings behind a mask of hostility, but in truth, I found her glamorous. Secretly, I would have liked sometimes to be petted and made much of by her, as Anne often was.

"It's hilarious to hear her prattling endlessly about that ratty old castle of hers, all in the tongue of a farmhand," said Juliana.

"And then she follows Master Manham round like a sad little spaniel," said Katherine, beginning to laugh. "I'm sure he doesn't notice, but it's so humiliating. It would be a kind deed to tell her. I'm almost tempted to teach her a lesson myself."

How unfair! I nearly burst out of the privy to have it out with her, but then I remembered how dreadful it would be if they knew that I was eavesdropping. In my uncertainty, I shifted upon my seat and a floorboard groaned. It sounded as loud as a cannon. I froze.

Luckily, the stable lads chose that moment to bring one of the horses into the yard below our window, and the distracting noises from outside saved me from detection.

"Indeed, she thinks she knows it all!" Katherine now ran on. "But I know for a fact that despite her talk of grand marriages and alliances, she understands nothing about how to win a husband and make him happy."

I frowned.

I had to admit to myself that my habit of showing off about my family's grandeur was unattractive.

But I also wondered if there were some arcane lessons in making a man fall in love with you that Katherine and the older girls had learned, and that

I had not. Perhaps these were the lessons given privately by the duchess herself, in the evenings after dinner, when only a few chosen older girls were invited to withdraw with her into her own chamber.

At the same time, though, I was relieved to hear Katherine and Juliana clattering out of the room in their leather slippers, with the workbox or book or whatever it was they had sought, and slamming the door behind them. I crept out of my humiliating hiding place and lay down upon the unmade nest of my bed.

What does she know, anyway? I thought. I rolled on my side, letting a hot tear spill down my cheek and soak into my pillow. *I bet I do know more than her about how to make a man happy.*

While all the girls claimed to be passionately in love with Master Manham, our music master, I had reason to believe that among all the girls at Trumpton, he liked me best of all.

Chapter 11

The Music Lesson

1537

When eventually it all came out, it was said that the old duchess had been very short-sighted — as indeed she was, tapping away with her white stick. But that's not what they meant. They meant that she had failed to see what kind of behaviour was going on in her very own house, beneath her very own pointy aristocratic nose.

With Master Manham, it began like this. I went, as usual, to the closet for my lute lesson. Now, for a well-born young lady to be all alone with a man, even a servant of a rank lower than her own, everyone knows that it should not happen.

But at Trumpton that's how all of us girls had our individual music lessons, with Master Manham, in the little painted closet upstairs. And everyone knows too that closets are rooms where secrets should be kept safe. One secret that had somehow slipped out of this particular closet during the course of someone's lesson was Master Manham's Christian name, and we all learned that it was Francis. A scratched "F" appeared on the diamond-shaped pane of one of the windows of the maidens' chamber, with a raggedy heart drawn around it.

One day I was in the closet at my lute lesson with Trumpton Hall's most popular teacher, and we were playing the song "Oh, My Love." I have not got a beautiful clear singing voice like Anne's, but most of the teachers at Trumpton had by now told me that I am quick-witted. This was news. Our more formal lessons seemed easy to me, but I'd assumed that was because I had already covered many of their topics with my father. Anyway, it seemed to me simple stuff to write a tune down upon my page, and then to play it, my fingers moving almost mechanically up and down the lute's board.

"Oh, *my love*," I warbled, sounding more than a little like a mewling cat. I never attempted to sing well in my lessons. I'm afraid that if I cannot excel, I am often guilty of not attempting a task at all. In fact, I usually succeeded in yowling so badly that Master Manham laughed and begged me to stop, and then I would distract him from the lesson with chat instead.

"Oh, *my beauty*," I continued, as the song dictated. At that, Master Ginger, the household's orange tom, suddenly put his face around the door, for all the world as if I had summoned him in cat language.

Master Manham and I both burst out laughing at the same time. Master Ginger, with his ears raggedy from fighting, was the very opposite of beautiful.

"Oh dear, he took my singing for that of a lady cat!"

This started Master Manham off once more, and I had to join in, a little ruefully. As our giggles subsided, Master Manham stepped close to me. "Never mind," he said more seriously. "You may not have a beautiful voice, but you have a gift for musical composition. As does the king himself."

He did not ask me to play on. I wondered what he was waiting for.

When he spoke next, it was in much quieter tones. "And you have such pretty dimples too!" he said.

I felt myself blushing and hung my head to hide it. He said this kind of thing quite often, to many of the girls. But then his smile faded. Dipping his own head to meet my averted gaze and looking at me intently, he placed his hand over my fingers as if to reposition them on the lute. "Oh, my beauty," he said, looking into my eyes.

I stared back, transfixed. His eyes were a warm brown and lay beneath an adorable curl of auburn hair that sprang from his forehead. I felt, as I had often done before, an absurd desire to smooth it flat with my hand. One of the reasons I liked him was that his hair, although darker, was so close to the colour of my own. But I sat quite still, and my insides suddenly turned to a jelly junket. He seemed close, far too close to me. I lowered my eyes. The room had grown very hot and still.

All too soon, the moment had passed. Master Ginger slipped out with a parting flick of his tail, and Master Manham quickly struck up the song again, proceeding with the lesson quite as usual.

But something had changed. That night at supper I felt myself sparkling a little more brightly than usual, and I made Anne laugh so much that most unusually the duchess herself had to tell the meek Sweet to behave in a more maidenly manner.

All this had taken place a few weeks before I overheard Katherine and Juliana talking about me in the maidens' chamber.

And that very same evening, I had it triumphantly confirmed that, despite what Katherine had said, Francis Manham had special feelings for me.

After dinner the whole household went outside. It was a balmy evening, and the big round moon hung low over the lavender bushes. All the girls took a little paper lantern, and we laughingly performed the rather fancy dance that Monsieur Bleu called "The Nine Muses." We ourselves usually called it "The Nine Elephants" after the beasts of the forest with their long drooping noses, as we had to bow right down with an arm extended to touch the very floor. But I think that all of us, that night, for the first time appreciated the symmetry and grace of the dance. So we swayed and bowed and swung our lanterns high and low in the evening dusk.

The duchess's gentlemen and gentlewomen and all the other masters and mistresses burst out clapping, and we ran, our spirits high, out into the woods. It was a glorious hour, one of my best ever times at Trumpton.

In the woods I myself began to perform a silly dance I'd made up. "I *tremble, I tremble!*" I sang, "I *fawn, I fawn!*" Matching my actions to my words, I bowed down before the fallen trunk where Katherine Howard sat. All the girls were laughing, and even she cracked a smile.

"Oh, King Henry, King Henry," I continued, "*without you I'm forlorn. Do place your royal foot upon my gentle fawnish neck and . . . crush me.*" It was delightful to have everyone applauding my clowning, and the goddess-like Katherine herself playfully pretended to wring my head from my neck.

Then the other members of the household followed us through the trees, and it was no longer safe to poke fun at Old Trembles. We all went on together, but the path was too narrow for the whole group. It split and split again. Soon I was walking along with Master Manham just an arm's length away from my side, and I was surprised and pleased to find that we were a little apart from the rest of the company. We pressed on through the glimmering woodland, following the laughing voices ahead of us. Occasionally, he lifted a trail of ivy or a bramble out of my path, bowing nonsensically low as I went by.

Then suddenly we passed from moonlight into a dark place, and I stumbled a little. Immediately, his hands were round my waist and—amazing sensation—his warm lips were nuzzling against mine.

I felt that all the blood in my veins had turned into quicksilver.

Only a moment later, though, Alice and the rest came running back in our direction. We heard the call to return to the hall and trooped back indoors. The spell was snapped.

That night, our room was full of laughter and gossip until the early hours. But one voice—mine—was completely silent. I was full to the brim with happiness, and I felt that life at Trumpton held nothing but pleasure and promise.

We had talked so often of love in the maidens' chamber that I had no doubt that I was experiencing it for myself. I began to imagine the life that I'd lead with Francis as my husband, thinking of new ways to make him happy every day, all the children we'd have . . .

There was only one tiny lurking worry in my mind. If I were to marry a music teacher, how could I save Stoneton from ruin?

Chapter 12

The Closet, Midnight

1537

Although I had made such a cold, bad start with Katherine, after the silly evening in the woods, we began slowly to approach each other, like the dog and the lion warily circling round each other before either pouncing or parting. I think we both recognised that we shared a sharpness the other girls didn't possess.

"Anne Sweet is sweet," she said to me in a whisper, while Anne was simpering at one of Master Manham's jokes, "but she's a little insipid, don't you find?"

I secretly shared her opinion, but then Anne had been so kind so me. Feeling more than a little guilty, I cocked my head to the side, as if to say "maybe."

And when Anne wanted to sit next to me at dinner, I told her that Mistress Katherine Howard had already reserved the seat.

But I must admit that Katherine could be devilish. There was the time, for example, when we were all learning how best to wash and starch fine lace. She clumsily ripped the lace collar in her own basin — and I caught sight of her quickly switching it with the garment in Juliana's basin while Juliana was out of the room. Katherine caught me looking, gave her lazy smile, and gently raised her finger to her lips. Such was the power of her personality that my initial shock gave way to the cosy feeling that we now shared a secret.

All the girls wanted to look like my cousin Katherine, with her creamy skin and her limpid blue eyes that beamed like lanterns. In the maidens' chamber, she often used to coach us all in how to throw what she called "killing" glances. She was convinced that if you looked at a man in her special narrow-eyed way, he would be sure to fall in love with you. But this I could not believe.

"Nonsense!" I cried out one day, when her queenly ways and beneficent advice had begun to grate. "Gentlemen like to hear what you have to say. They like girls with spirit. They don't just want to look at smiling dummies. They might as well just look at a painting if that were all."

"And did your *betrothed husband the viscount* like what you had to say, my lady Eliza?"

I did not answer her and made as if I had not heard. I flumped down angrily upon my bed and pretended to read a letter from Aunt Margaret as if it interested me greatly.

"At least I have *had* an offer of marriage," I muttered into the folded paper. "I'm the only one here who knows what it actually feels like."

Everyone copied the way Katherine did her hair, coiled round the back of her head almost like a crown. Despite my crossness with her, I could still enjoy the jealous looks that Juliana and Anne gave me when Katherine called me one morning to sit on her own bed so that she could braid my long but rather straggling locks.

As we sat and chatted, I nonchalantly said that I had seen and not particularly admired the hair of Queen Jane at Westmorland House. As I had only seen her in the distance and by twilight, I would perhaps have been better advised not to mention it. But I knew that Katherine was violently interested, as I was, in court matters. And there was so little that I knew which she did not.

"Was it rich and black?" she asked idly, her fingers busily flicking back and forth with my hair.

"Yes, it was black," I confirmed, "but I think her women could have dressed it better."

At that she pulled my braid so as to turn my face towards her.

"You are such a little liar, Eliza," she said good-humouredly. "Everyone knows that Queen Jane is blonde."

I felt myself colour up, but my stubbornness refused to let me back down and say I had been mistaken.

She finished my hair in silence, but it became torture rather than pleasure.

✳

Even so, I longed more than anything to brag to Katherine about the kiss I had received from Master Manham in the woods and to ask her what it meant. Oddly — and confusingly — my next lute lesson passed exactly as usual, as if nothing had happened. I began to fear that perhaps indeed I didn't know how to make a man fall in love with me, as Katherine herself had claimed.

But then, one evening, she and I were the very last to leave the Great Chamber, where we'd been setting the banqueting table. We had learned that afternoon from old Abigail how to position the goblets, the grapes, the sweetmeats, and the forks for best effect. Our table, the fruit of our work, was a marvellous sight with its sugar sculptures, candied violets, and scattered rose petals. It seemed a terrible shame that no visitors from court were due, to marvel at it and sample its pleasures. Katherine and I lingered on as the light faded, admiring our efforts and giving a final, unnecessary polish to glasses and cordial bottles.

She herself looked wondrously beautiful as she turned her head this way and that, her profile with its coronet of hair silhouetted against the setting sun.

"Here's a table to woo a lover!" Katherine said with pride, as she caressed the fine inlaid marble surface with her hand.

"Indeed," I said, "and how would you continue to woo him once he'd eaten and drunk?" I was emboldened by the dusk and our isolation in the darkening room.

"Well, my dear little Carrot Top," she said, "I would rip off all his clothes!"

I tried not to look shocked, for I knew that she was teasing and toying with me. But I did understand that men and woman wanted to touch each other when they were in love. I felt that way about Master Manham. I put up my hands to stroke my own new hairdo, pretending to myself that I looked almost as good as Katherine did, and hummed a little tune. A careful listener might have detected that the melody was "Oh, My Love."

"Oh!" Katherine said. "I can see that someone fancies herself to be in love. Who is the lucky man, I wonder?"

At that, though, I kept my own counsel. I knew that to tell her would give her power over me, and I was not sure that I wanted to take that step. Instead I gave what I hoped was a supercilious smile. "Wouldn't you like to know?" I said.

"Aha!" said Katherine. "You forget that I have ways of finding out. No secret is safe from me." At that she swept out of the chamber. I looked at the door she had just closed, annoyed. Why did she always have to know everyone's secrets and to be so annoyingly right about everything?

But then I imagined Master Manham opening the door and coming over to join me at the banqueting table. Soon I was lost in a pleasant reverie.

It was later that same fateful evening, and I was sitting at my embroidery frame in the dusk, when one of the serving girls came over to me with a slip of parchment folded very small. Little Em, the smallest and least impressive maid, was known throughout the household for being terrified of everyone and everything. She was half simple, poor thing, and couldn't follow even the easiest of instructions unless you repeated them slowly.

"For you, m'm, from him," she mumbled, quickly backing off and departing.

I set the note aside, as if I couldn't have cared less what was in it. But my heart was pounding so loud in my chest that I was sure Anne could hear it from across the room. I forced myself to put a few more stitches into the peacock I was working on, before nonchalantly telling the girls that I was going to fetch a lamp against the gloom.

Once in the dim but deserted hall, I fumbled as if my life depended upon it to open up the paper, trembling with both excitement and trepidation. I already half knew what it would say. There were just three words, in the loopy hand so familiar from the instructions written in the margins of my music books.

The closet, midnight, they read.

I could hardly swallow my supper when the time came, and when I knelt beside my bed, the words of my evening prayer simply wouldn't come to mind.

I knew that I should not meet Francis alone until we were betrothed, and that to follow his instructions would make God angry. But surely Francis wanted me to go to the closet in order to tell me that he loved me? And then it would be all right. I was so excited and nervous that, yes, I trembled like a fawn.

Never had the late-night chat seemed more trivial, and never did the girls seem to take such a long time to drop off to sleep. There was the usual coming and going to the privy, the running down to the maidservants' room with forgotten instructions about clothes for tomorrow, and the laughing out the window at the stable boys.

I closed my eyes as tight as I could and put my fingers in my ears.

Finally, what seemed like years later, I heard the stable clock *bong* twelve. I immediately opened my eyes and sat bolt upright. It was much darker now, but it was only summer darkness, with a gleam of evening still present. There was enough light to see quite well as I padded between the lumpy piles of girl and coverlet.

Up the stairs I went. A faint memory pushed its way into my thoughts: the recollection of another summer night when I had climbed a staircase to an adventure that had turned out very badly indeed.

But I continued with my stealthy climb.

The door of the closet stood very slightly ajar, and inside I could see the gleam of a candle. I nearly went back then, back to safety, back to the maidens' chamber where I belonged.

But some devilry that has always been inside me pressed me forward into the room.

And there, upon a carpet on the floor, lay a tangle of arms and legs. There was not one person present; there were two. There lay Francis Manham indeed, but in his arms lay Katherine. Her dark, tangled hair was loose and lay fanned out all around their heads as if it were a pillow for them both. They looked cosy, almost domestic, with their limbs entwined. I took in the fact that they had been drinking wine, and that he was in the act of popping a strawberry into her mouth.

They were so relaxed together that I knew at once they'd come here like this many, many times before.

Nor did they seem at all put out as they looked up and saw my startled face. The worst humiliation of all was when they started to laugh, he rather shamefacedly, she with wild abandon.

"Oh, Francis, you were right after all!"

Katherine choked out the words between peals of laughter, sitting up now and clapping her hands. "You win the wager!" she said. "I really didn't think she'd come, but she must be crazy for you, just like you said!"

"Crazy!" was the word that rang in my ears as I rushed out of the closet and back towards my bed, fiery red and sweaty with shame.

Chapter 13

Would You Not Like to Be a Maid of Honour?

1539

Of course my time at Trumpton was tainted after that. I could hardly look at Master Manham. He, too, acted stiffly with me.

At our next lute lesson, I asked him outright what was happening. "I may be just a foolish northerner," I said, "but are you quite as friendly with all the girls as you are with Katherine?" I said nothing of our kiss in the woods, because obviously it had meant nothing to him.

"I don't know what you mean, Mistress Camperdowne," he said, shifting his weight from foot to foot. "I treat all the ladies as I believe they like to be treated."

When I stared at him, he stared right back, implacable, impregnable. I knew that I would get no further explanation or apology. I turned to the window with a tight little smile, looking through it without seeing the garden outside. My mind sought something—anything—to ease its burning pain, but nothing came into my head at all apart from a desperate desire to show him that I was calm and cool.

With Katherine, it felt like we had gone right back to the start, to the very day she had been so cruel to me upon my arrival. When I saw her laughing, or bossing the other girls, or flirting with the teachers, I felt I was looking at the devil in the form of a girl. Why could not everyone else see what I saw? To me she was cold, heartless, egotistical, and arrogant. I wondered how I could ever have let her plait my hair, and kept as much out of her way as I could.

I took to roaming about in the gardens by myself, sometimes playing melancholy airs on my lute. Once again I felt that I was an alien, an outsider in this place. The duchess herself did little to relieve this. As I become one of the older girls, and others took the places of Anne and me as the littlest, she took me into her withdrawing room and told me, in the most frighteningly technical terms, how to perform the duties of a wife and how best to bear a man's child.

The duchess's clinical detachment made my heart throb a little with a sensation I had not felt for some time: that of missing my mother. This should have been her task, performed with warmth and sympathy, not coldness. And my sore heart made me think of my aunt anew. Although Aunt Margaret was strict and practical too, I knew, if only from Henny, that she cared about me. Even if the duchess did care, she certainly did not show it.

The duchess, though, did admire my progress as her pupil, and I knew she was pleased with me. One summer's evening, nearly two whole years later, I was kneeling before her, peeking up at her demurely through my eyelashes as we had been taught, and raising in my hand the cup of cordial for which she had called.

I artfully allowed my sleeve to fall back to reveal the graceful turn of my wrist, exactly as Monsieur Bleu had prescribed. This time, though, she failed to take the drink. Instead, she grasped my wrist and drew me up to my feet to stand before her.

"Child, how old are you now? Fifteen years?" she asked. I nodded. She frequently addressed me as "child," in a strange echo of my aunt Margaret, but sometimes I feared that she did it only because she had genuinely forgotten my name. "I congratulate you. You have been a very quick learner, as accomplished as girls two years older than yourself. We have nothing more to teach you here. You are now an elegant young lady, an asset to our extended family, and ready to go to grace the royal court."

My eyebrows arched with surprise and pleasure, despite my efforts to keep them down and not to furrow my forehead. I hoped that the older girls to whom she had referred included my cousin Katherine. My mind ran ahead. Perhaps one day, at court, I might even put her into the shade by becoming the court's most popular and sought-after maid of honour.

I knew that the treaty had recently been signed for the king's new marriage. Queen Jane, whom I had glimpsed at Westmorland, had died in childbirth, horrific news to all of us who would be expected to bear heirs to our husbands when the time came. The king had been left bereft and miserable, but we had heard that he'd recovered to the extent of contemplating marriage to the German princess, Anne of Cleves.

New maids of honour would of course be required for the household of the new queen, and it was widely expected that the Duchess of Northumberland would be consulted for her recommendation. After so much training and debating and waiting, all of us girls longed to go to see the palaces and pageantry of the court. I discovered that I was actually holding my breath in anticipation of her next words.

"I am sending Mistress Howard to court," she now said, "as a maid of honour to the new queen." A stab of jealousy and hatred made me wince.

Despite her poor eyesight, the duchess did see some things quite clearly, and she obviously noticed my reaction. "Tell me," she continued, "I am curious about you and her. You two have so much in common — you're cousins — but you've hardly spoken to each other these past two years. Why are my brightest girls enemies, not friends? Your looks are so different that you cannot compete on the grounds of beauty."

She had no need to add that Katherine was beautiful and that I was . . . not. Although Anne Sweet was always bubbling up with compliments for my clothes and my style, as we dressed up of an evening in the maidens' chamber, everyone wanted to be luxuriantly plump and sloe-eyed like Katherine, not willowy and gingery like me.

I couldn't think what to say. "Your Grace, I *am* indeed most fond of Mistress Howard" was my final, if inadequate, answer. I clasped my hands in front of me to keep them still, eager to give nothing else away.

"Well, keep yourself to yourself, then!" the duchess said smartly. "There is indeed precious little room for friendships at court. But tell me, would you not like to be a maid of honour too?"

Now my careful courtly mask slipped. "Indeed I would!" I burst out. I knew that I should not bounce on my toes like a child, but I could not help it. "I would like of all things to go to court."

"Well, go you shall," she said. "But there is a final task here for you before you become a maid of honour. You should study the German language. Your new mistress will need all the help she can get."

I had never before thought that a princess, shortly to become a queen, would require help, especially not the help of a useless gawky creature like me. But I would help her, I decided, as best as I possibly could. And certainly I would be kinder and more helpful than that beast Katherine.

Part Three

At Court

Chapter 14

A Cold Welcome

1539
ELIZABETH IS FIFTEEN . . .

So, only a couple of weeks later, we said goodbye to Trumpton Hall. Between the layers of clothing in our trunks lay many inexpertly made lavender bags, gifts from our cousins, and we had with us a basket of autumn apples for the journey.

"Goodbye, girls! You may come to join my household when I am married!" Katherine called confidently out of the wagon's rear opening.

"Enough of that!" snapped the old duchess, turning as if to slap heads as shrieks and giggles arose from our former companions. But the hint of a smile played around the creases of her mouth, for Katherine, her favourite, was always to be indulged. The last sound we heard as the wagon moved off was Anne calling out, "Godspeed, Eliza! Godspeed, Katherine! Oh, I wish I were going with you!"

I would have rather chosen any one of the other girls as a travelling companion. But I knew that the rest of them were jealous as Katherine and I had packed our bags to go away together, and an uneasy truce seemed to have settled itself between us. It was as if we both realised that while we may have been at odds at Trumpton, an ally would be more useful than an enemy in the unknown world of the court.

"My God, I'm looking forward to fishing in deeper waters!" Katherine said, with her slow and confidential smile, flopping back on the cushions as our journey began. She lazily stretched out her arm along the back of the seat, taking up all the room.

"Are you going to be a *king*-fisher?" I asked, trying to ignore the fact that I had either to ask her to move or shrink myself uncomfortably into the corner.

"Goodness!" Katherine said in mock surprise. "Our little Eliza just made quite a grown-up joke."

At that, we both shivered with sheer excitement.

But then I told myself, sternly, to calm down. This wasn't a pleasure jaunt or a holiday. It was my duty now to grow up and settle down and find a husband suitable not only for myself but for Stoneton. It was imperative that Katherine did not immediately snap up the best candidate for herself.

Long hours later, the gloss had faded from the day. We had passed the time sleeping and eating our apples, and it was nearly nightfall when we finally drew near the Palace of Greenwich. The king had many palaces, and we would live in whichever one currently pleased him most, travelling with him as he moved on. We had never been to any palace, let alone this particularly fine one on the banks of the wide River Thames at Greenwich, and neither of us wished to acknowledge the nervousness we felt as our new life began.

It was well into the evening when we approached the tall brick gatehouse of the palace, its wooden gates firmly shut. It seemed awfully quiet as the horses came to a halt, because our ears had been hammered by the sound of hoof-beats for many hours.

Nothing happened. There was more silence.

Eventually, a tiny door in the big gate creaked a little way open, and a porter came out. Our servant had to climb down and speak to him for a long time before he slowly began to swing back the gates.

"What's going on?" Katherine called out to our man.

The reply was disheartening.

"That stupid fellow did not recognise your names," he said. "I had to explain that her grace the duchess had sent you." Katherine and I avoided each other's gaze.

In the courtyard, we tumbled stiffly out from our seats, and a red-faced, harassed-looking man perfunctorily welcomed us to Greenwich. "If you run to the Hall, there should still be supper," he said. But before we could ask which way to go, he was busy instructing our outriders to move forward so that the luggage could be more easily unloaded by a silent and weary-looking team of footmen.

So, giggling a little from fatigue and tension, Katherine and I made our way through several courtyards. Somehow we even ended up hand in hand. This was a vast warren of a building, like seventeen Stonetons all in one. Even by the dim light of candles in horn lanterns placed at intervals on the stone ledges of windows, we could see that it was richly and brightly coloured, with painting and gilding and heraldic devices crowding every surface.

Finally, after many twists and turns, we approached a fine doorway that seemed fit for a Great Hall. As we drew near, two tall figures stepped forward from the shadows. Two bulky men dressed in red, with long spears in their hands, barred our way.

"Who seeks entrance to the king's chambers?"

The request was barked out rather than spoken, and the two men had sent their weapons flying forth as if one clockwork mechanism powered them both.

"Oh, sirs!" said Katherine. "We are new here and seek only supper." I could tell that we weren't supposed to have spoken to these grumpy giants. One of them briefly nodded to the left, down the cloister, and off we ran, sniggering from embarrassment, like the schoolgirls we no longer were.

The Great Hall, when we found it, was a disappointment. Yes, it was enormous, and we could hardly see its rafters through the smoke of the braziers burning at intervals along its length. But the long tables were nearly empty. A rowdy group of young men, rolling dice and drinking, sat at one end. They emitted a volley of crude wolf whistles as we entered, then they proceeded completely to ignore us.

We sat hesitantly, and with some reluctance a serving man finally came and poured us ale and threw down some slices of beef before us. We hadn't unpacked our knives from our baggage and were somewhat at a loss how to begin eating without using our unwashed hands.

"My ladies!" It was the first friendly voice we'd heard. "What brings you to this rough place at this late hour?"

I turned to see a tall thin boy, about Katherine's own age, I thought, bringing us a basin of water and a towel. He had yellowish hair and a friendly, if lopsided, smile. I sensed that Katherine was smiling back as if he'd offered us a jug of rare hippocras rather than merely a finger bowl.

"Ned Barsby, at your service," he said, doffing his cap in a casually elegant manner that would have made Monsieur Bleu swoon.

Master Barsby told us that he was a Page of the Presence, and that it was his job to strike the flint to light the fire in the king's own chambers. He was, in fact, not supposed to be out here in the common dining hall, but he'd had a night off duty and felt the urge to roll a die or two.

"I'm really no good at these court pursuits like gambling or drinking," he explained, "but I have to do my best to fit in with the other animals on this particular farm."

Right on cue, two of the shouty young men in the corner started grappling with each other, drunkenly play-fighting while their fellows egged them on.

Our new friend raised his eyebrows, cast a disparaging glance towards them, and turned back to us.

"When I saw two pretty new girls," he said warmly, "I thought it would have been unmannerly not to come over for some more civilised conversation."

In a moment, he was lending us his own knife and serving us salt. He was so easy to talk to that soon we were chatting like old friends. Or at least Katherine was, as she explained all about our lives so far and our purpose in coming to court.

Meanwhile I looked carefully at Ned Barsby. His doublet was very well cut and smart, but it was just a plain dark blue and not fastened up properly. His hair was a little longer than I was used to, but it fell negligently across his forehead in a manner that seemed comfortable rather than vain. He sat with us as if he had all the time in the world, interlacing his fingers and cracking his knuckles. The tension in my stomach began gradually to unwind.

Although Katherine was still piping on with her rather banal description of our journey and how awfully long it had been, my feelings bubbled up. "Do you know," I burst out, unable to help myself, "I thought that the court would be more glamorous than this!"

Master Barsby smiled at me instead of Katherine for what felt like the first time. "Ah, but that's court life for you," he said. "Half glamour, half squalor. I'm the squalor," he quickly added. "You two are clearly the glamour." He explained that we would normally have our meals in the Great Chamber, with the other ladies of the court, and regretted that standards of hospitality had fallen so far short that nobody other than himself had come to welcome us.

When we had finished eating, he led us through the doorway into the Chamber itself, dark and deserted that night, but richly hung with tapestries.

Katherine, of course, was monopolising Master Barsby, so I resigned myself to being neglected. Taking up a candle, I examined the walls more closely. The light picked out what seemed to be threads of gold. I gasped as I realised that I was looking at a fine tapestry elephant, with an armed hero on his back, in blue and green and scarlet. I had never seen anything as beautiful in my life.

And suddenly Master Barsby was by my side, taking my elbow in a warm grip and steering me across the room. "I see you appreciate art," he said.

"Come to see the latest work of Master Holbein." He led me confidently across the vast floor as if he could navigate blindfolded, while I would have tripped and hesitated in the darkness. Standing on an easel at the other end of the room was a painting covered with a red cloth.

Master Barsby looked both ways, but there was nobody present but the three of us. He quickly tweaked the cloth from the easel, and, as he lifted his candlestick, we saw before us a beautiful woman, eyes downcast, a strange gauzy hood on her head. She was a picture of passive, serene virtue.

"My ladies," he said. "Meet your mistress, the future Queen Anne."

Chapter 15

Trickery and Flirtation

1539

Master Ned Barsby told us that the king had fallen in love with this portrait. "It has reassured our master," he told us, "that the Princess of Cleves is beautiful. It's important that our queen be wondrously fair as well as providing England with an alliance with her German home state."

"But the lady Anne Boleyn wasn't wondrously fair, was she? It is said that she was almost ugly."

Master Barsby gave my cousin a cool look. "Well, madam," he said, "it's not for me to judge. But it's also said she had great skills of trickery and flirtation.

The king has chosen his fourth wife so carefully because he has been deceived before."

I could see Katherine drinking in all this information, and I was doing the same thing myself. My shoulders slumped. I realised that Katherine herself was flirtatious and treacherous and wondrously fair as well. Surely even the former queen Anne Boleyn would have been outclassed by my cousin? Katherine would certainly have her pick of the court's unmarried men. How could I compete?

But Master Barsby was smiling at me now, his eyes sparkling in the light of his candle. "May I advise you, madam, to keep your counsel," he added to my cousin, speaking kindly but decisively, "just as Mistress Eliza here does? The old queens are no longer spoken of at court."

I had done the right thing in keeping quiet, then, and Master Barsby had noticed.

"Anyway, it's all about the Princess Anne of Cleves now," Master Barsby went on, turning back to the picture with such enthusiasm that a little wax splashed from his candle and burned his fingers. He yelped and swore, but quickly brushed it off and continued talking.

"His Majesty the King visits Master Holbein's picture each morning. He unveils it and talks to it, wishing her good morning. He'll tell any of the courtiers present in the Chamber about her beauty, her powerful father, the fine Protestant religion they have in Germany, and the desirability that all men should marry. You'll hear him yourselves. 'Children!' he tells us, practically every day. 'A brother for my baby son, Edward! That's what we require at this court.'"

A *baby son . . . we need a baby son.* Master Barsby's words echoed in my mind when I finally lay in our hard new bed, as tired as a dog, next to a gently snoring Katherine. I was determined to become a vital, valued part of the court and to take all its concerns to my own heart.

The next day, our first morning as maids of honour, we were summoned to the chambers of the Countess of Malpas. Small, blonde-haired, and constantly smiling, this countess was our supervisor and would assign us our duties. As she spelled them out to us in her room high in the inner red-brick gatehouse, they seemed almost laughably simple. Her chamber's windows looked both ways to provide a good view of not one but two courtyards. "I like to lodge here," she told us, "because up here in my eyrie I can see the comings and goings of all my young ladies."

She pointed out to us the window of the king's own private bedchamber, which lay directly opposite, and told us how she would watch for the extinguishing of the light, which signalled that service for the day was over.

"And in the morning," she said, "we have to watch for the moment that the window is opened. The king's bedchamber servants open it to refresh the room once the king has gone forth. That's the signal for us to be on duty."

She told us that when the king came out of his own private bedchamber and met members of his court, he wanted entertainment.

"He needs his senior courtiers to sit with him, laugh at his jokes, compliment him on his performances on the lute or the recorder, or tell him dirty stories," she said with a trilling laugh.

"I don't understand what we are actually supposed to do," I complained. "Do we just stand there?"

But the countess was charmingly vague about this.

"You are to be *an ornament to the court*, my dears," she said, "looking pretty and delighting the men. And ravishing beauties you both are too," she added, kindly including me in her statement. "You will not be many years as maids of honour, for you will both soon find rich husbands." At this I saw Katherine wriggle her shoulders with glee.

"The most important thing," the countess went on, "is to watch and to wait and to be ready. You will know opportunity when you see it."

I was left feeling a little mystified and a little anxious. When should I start hunting for a husband? How should I go about it? I was not quite sure, and I didn't like to ask Katherine. She would surely laugh in my face.

But I must admit I enjoyed the dressing session that followed with the countess's tiring woman. She made us get out all our gowns, and she sent half of them to the seamstresses to be altered. "The neckline needs to be a little lower, to show more of your creamy shoulders," she said to Katherine of her red velvet. "And this one is far too loose, Mistress Camperdowne," she told me of my cornflower silk. "It will have to be taken in. The king will want to be able to see what shape you are—you can't wear a sack."

She also showed us the casket from which we could borrow jewels, which we were meant to rotate so that all the maids of honour looked freshly magnificent. It was thrilling to handle and examine such a great store of treasures, but after a while I began to think that there were almost too many of them. I hardly knew how to begin selecting which ones to wear. Perhaps it would be simpler just to stick with my mother's pearls.

Finally, the countess gave us a little more court insight about the king. We clustered close to her, as if she were revealing state secrets. "He has to sit with his leg raised on a cushion," she said solemnly, "for he has a painful ulcer. He's had it for four years now, since he fell off his horse. What a rider he used to be! And an archer! It's sad to see him missing his sports."

"Well, we hear that there's at least one sport he still enjoys," said Katherine. I looked at her aghast. It was all very well for Katherine and I to make crude remarks when we were alone, but in front of our supervisor?

But the countess took her perfectly seriously.

"Yes," she said, almost reverently, "our master the king is still a great lover of the ladies."

Chapter 16

A Bold Ginger Kitten

1539

And so, two days later, wearing our gowns court-fashion, we met the king.

Far from being in my shift, as I had been when I glimpsed him at Westmorland House, I was confident that I had never before been so becomingly dressed. On this first day of court duty, the long-awaited day when we would take our places in palace life, we had risen at dawn to get ready.

Then, tense and nervous, we waited with the Countess of Malpas in her room. I sat bolt upright in my blue silk, trying to look worldly and nonchalant and yet at the same time trying not to crease my dress.

"He's only a man with a bad leg!" I mouthed the words silently to myself as I smoothed the fabric with my hands. But the king was also the man whose picture I had seen on the first page of the Bible, laying down the law to all the bishops in the land. I could tell that Katherine was on edge too as she positioned and repositioned her pendant, lowering it a little farther down its chain.

There was no escaping the fact that we had spent a very long time — years, in fact — preparing for this day.

We were both watching like hunting hawks when the king's bedchamber window across the courtyard popped open and a cheerful hand flapped out. "That's Ned Barsby," the countess explained, "giving us our signal to attend." Suddenly moving with great speed, she scurried down the twisting staircase. We followed her across the courtyard and up the stairs into the Great Chamber. The flurry of motion after sitting still made my heart flap like the wings of a swan trying to lift itself into flight.

The countess thrust us into position, standing meekly in front of the magnificent elephant tapestry, with our hands clasped in front of us. "Lower your eyes," she hissed, as she whisked into line beside us.

Reluctantly obeying her, I cast my eyes to the floor, so I was unable to see the king approach.

I did, however, hear a door being thrown open and the loud *thunk* of those massive yeomen guards presenting their weapons. There was a heavy step and the *thump* of a stick. We sensed that a large, hulking figure, gaudy in cloth of gold, had paused before us. Instantly, we fell to the floor in the deep abasement Monsieur Bleu had taught us for royalty. My gown now fitted me so tightly that I had to suck in my breath to get down low, and I definitely heard a stitch pop. When we rose, I sensed the king's eyes travelling up and down our bodies, for all the world as if he were a farmer looking at cows at a market.

When his gaze reached Katherine's chest, I saw him smile. But he said nothing at all.

The silence seemed to me to be growing uncomfortable. "The Duchess of Northumberland has sent us from Trumpton Hall, Your Majesty," I said.

At once the countess shushed me. "Excuse her, Your Majesty, she does not yet know not to speak first."

"Ah, that ancient crone Northumberland has sent us a bold ginger kitten, I see!"

I'd expected a booming, deep voice, but it was shallow and croaky, as if it belonged to a much older man.

But at his words I could not contain myself. Gibes about red hair from the red-headed king himself!

"*Ginger*," I said loudly, "is a fine colour for the hair, sir, if I may be so bold."

There might have been a stifled yelp of laughter from one of the gentlemen standing behind the king. But a sharp pain in my ankle told me that the countess had actually given me a vicious little kick. I tensed myself, aghast. Had I been too personal?

He glanced at me briefly, but then his gaze went quickly back to Katherine. She was still deep down in her curtsey, her head demurely bent forward, her shoulders pulled back, a picture of obedience. The king seemed deeply uninterested in the Duchess of Northumberland or the colour of hair. Spinning round abruptly, he went with his slow stomp to sit in the oriel window. I turned to my companions in some consternation and saw that Katherine was blushing and — to my mind — simpering. The Countess of Malpas was patting her arm approvingly.

Too late, I realised that I'd made a mistake. He'd simply wanted to look at us, not to talk. I would have to take this maid of honour business, which sounded so easy, more seriously than I'd thought.

Chapter 17

You Can Never Escape

1539

The elephant tapestry became an ally of mine, for I loved to examine its beautiful intricacies as the long hours went slowly forward. Our first day in the Great Chamber set the pattern for many to follow. At first I could hardly bear to admit to myself that life at court was boring, but so it was. It was tiring too, as we were constantly on our feet, always smiling, curtseying to the king and the other men who came and went. Sometimes they lingered, staring at Katherine in open admiration, but often they scarcely seemed to see us at all.

"We're not just sheep for sale," I would mutter under my breath if a gentleman paused by the tapestry for a long, leering look. But Katherine would shush me and smile ever more beatifically.

When we were off duty, though, in the afternoons when the king was in council or out riding, the palace became a delightful place. There was the best of everything for us: fine beef, hot water brought at once whenever we wanted to wash, plenty of firewood to keep our rooms cosy, and huge squashy floor cushions upon which we could loll and gossip with the other maids and ladies-in-waiting. We drank amber wine from delicate glass goblets and never gave a thought to how much anything cost.

"Look!" I said to Katherine. "The countess says we may borrow any of these books we like!"

"Oh, don't waste your time with books" came her dismissive answer. "I'm off to learn that new Italian song. There's no time for sitting around reading, you know." But in fact she spent the afternoon flirting with the singing man and not really learning the tune at all.

Even better than the palace's luxuries, though,

was a long-anticipated treat from home. At my urgent written requests sent back to Stoneton, my father had agreed that Henny could come down to the court to be my own tiring woman. Although we were servants ourselves, each maid of honour was in turn allowed to have up to three lesser personal servants. So I was half sick with excitement to see Henny again.

When finally the group of riders from Stoneton clattered into the palace courtyard, I could hardly restrain myself from leaping into Henny's arms. I could tell that she, too, wanted to give me a hug. Instead, though, she disguised her spontaneous lurch towards me as a comical pretence at having lost the use of her legs through sitting too long. Once we were back in my room, away from the eyes of the snooty serving men, we did have hours of chat and some happy tears.

I have to admit, though, that a certain awkward-ness quickly descended upon our relationship. When we were in company, Henny's accent to me sounded uncouth and uneducated, and I found her dresses embarrassingly out-of-date. I was grateful to Katherine for getting her own French tiring woman, Hortense, to take Henny in hand, forcing her to lace more tightly and to wear the white Dutch cap that all the older ladies wore to cover their offensively grey hair.

One day Master Barsby found me mooning about at the window of the Great Chamber, watching Henny in the courtyard below as she went to fetch firewood for our rooms. I noticed that she completely failed to bow, as she should have done, to the Lord Chamberlain when he went by. She looked just as if she were crossing our courtyard at Stoneton, pattens on her feet, skirt hoicked up, and her red meaty forearms showing. It made me tap my fingernails on the pane with annoyance.

"Having difficulty reconciling court and home?" he asked softly, as if he'd read my mind. "It happens to nearly everyone."

I did not wish to answer. "How long have you been at court?" I said, countering one question with another. Although I found him dangerously perceptive, Master Barsby did seem to be both knowledgeable and kind. It was a combination that I had already learned to be uncommon in the palace.

"Since I was twelve," he said, moving to stand elbow to elbow with me in the window bay. "I was sent here as a boy. I know all the wicked ways of the courtiers, but I can never really be one of them."

"Why not, Master Barsby?" I asked, turning to look at him. To me he seemed to be truly an integral part of the place, especially now, in his dark blue doublet, tossing his hair out of his blue eyes and smiling a little as he looked down at me. He was just a head taller than I was and pleasantly broad-shouldered and narrow-hipped. His doublet lacing was all awry, as usual, and I had to restrain myself from absently reaching out to put it right for him.

"I was born on the wrong side of the blanket," he said, ruefully rubbing the back of his head. "In short, I'm a bastard. My father may be an earl, but he never married my mother. And he has no need to make me his heir because he has my half-brothers from his countess for that. Unlike you, I have no real home to go back to."

At this I noticed that he gave a heavy sigh. It was

the first time he had seemed anything less than urbane and charming, and I found myself touching his sleeve in sympathy.

I already knew that many courtiers did pine for their homes. Indeed, only the other day I had come across the Countess of Malpas with pink rims around her blue eyes and her hair all undone. "What's the matter, my lady?" I'd said. "Have we displeased the king?" It was almost shocking to see her sad, as she was usually so relentlessly cheerful.

"Oh no, oh no," she said distractedly, pushing back her blonde hair. "It's just that I miss my littlest boy so much. He's at home in the country." She had no fewer than ten children, I knew, and her oldest son was with us at court. "As I had so many other children for the succession, I thought I would keep my last baby just for myself," she'd explained. "But I have hardly seen him since I was called into waiting." I remembered her words as I heard Master Barsby confess that his situation was almost worse. He had no one missing him, no one to miss.

"So . . ." I said slowly, "even though you've been at court for years, you don't really live here?"

Ned smiled but shifted his weight from foot to foot. This was getting to be the most serious conversation that we'd ever had. But he didn't make a joke of it as I'd thought he might.

"Well," he said slowly, rubbing his head again. I'd observed that he often did that when he was thinking. It left his hair standing up in spikes so that he looked like a little boy. "No one really lives here. It's not a home. It's a place of work. I may look like I'm at home here, but that's because of my job. You know that the king's page spends a lot of time in the king's company. I see much more of him than you maids of honour."

This was certainly true. And we'd heard gossip that when the door to his private apartments was safely closed, the king would burp and swear and drink and tease or wrestle with his gentlemen, getting to know them almost as if they were his friends, not his servants.

"Unlike you lot, though"—and here Ned swung his thumb towards the place by the tapestry where we maids of honour usually stood —"I can't get any higher. You can marry well and climb the ladder.

But I can never inherit my father's estate or hope to become a groom or a gentleman of the bedchamber."

"So you're not really a courtier — is that what you're saying?" I was a little shocked that he would admit to this, for being a part of the court seemed to me — in theory at least — to be the most desirable thing in England.

"Yes," he said, nodding seriously. "But then who is *really* one of the courtiers, as you put it?"

I widened my eyes, about to protest, but then I remembered the sadness of the countess.

"This place plays tricks on your mind," he said, as I reluctantly nodded back at him. "It all seems so wonderful, but it isn't real. Don't get drawn in too deeply, that's my advice. Do you know what they say?"

I shook my head, dumbly. With sudden and surprising grace, Ned leaned forward and used a forefinger to lift a curl of my hair away from my cheek. He put his lips so close to my ear that I could feel his warm breath. His whispered words thrilled but also chilled me.

"They say you can never escape."

Chapter 18

A Monkey and a Masque

1539

The next morning, I plaited my hair more carefully than usual and stole a little of Katherine's rouge to put some colour into my cheeks. I intended to be on duty a little early, hoping to catch Ned Barsby once again before the rest of the courtiers arrived in the Great Chamber.

I studiously avoided thinking about what Aunt Margaret might have said about my plan. I'd just received a letter from her enclosing a list of the values of the estates of all the king's eligible unmarried gentlemen, and of course Ned Barsby's name was not among them.

But thinking over our conversation of yesterday, I felt that Ned's revelations had made him my friend, perhaps the first male friend I'd ever had. Today I wanted to relax my guard with him, ask him stupid questions, maybe complain about the pompousness of the Lord Chamberlain.

I even rehearsed various opening gambits in my mind.

"What do you think, Ned, of the French ambassador?"

I mouthed the words to myself before the silver mirror in our bedchamber, peering at my reflection and trying to calculate whether my lips looked prettier open or closed. "He said that we maids of honour are frightful English frumps and that our hair and dresses would never be tolerated at the chic court of France!"

I had high hopes that Ned might disagree with the ambassador's views.

But the Countess of Malpas had other plans for our morning. When Katherine and I reached her room to have our outfits inspected before going on duty, it was full of commotion. The chamber was packed with all her servants, who were shaking with what looked like pain until I realised that it was actually suppressed laughter. They were wringing their hands, but the countess herself was wielding a broomstick. All of them were staring intently upwards at the carving over the window.

"Shh!" Lady Malpas hissed as we entered, wagging her one free hand behind her back at us to make us stand still. Everyone froze. Looking upwards myself, I spotted the bony arms and long curling tail of a living creature, clinging to the scallop shell positioned over the window. The countess moved forward stealthily before suddenly giving a great wallop with her brush. With a horrible, childlike scream, the creature hurled itself down from the window, catching at a tapestry on its way with what appeared to be fingers, then loped sideways to the door.

"Blessed Virgin protect us!" Lady Malpas was shaking her broom in rage. "That miserable monkey of Master Summers's has been drinking Thimble's milk again." Thimble was the countess's cat and much doted upon by his mistress.

Katherine and I exchanged nods of recognition.

We had heard about this famous monkey, which the courtiers found to be hilarious and exasperating in equal measure, but we had never before seen it. We'd often been told how it would steal the expensive imported figs brought out to tempt the king's appetite after dinner in full view of everyone, but acting out a pantomime parody of a light-fingered burglar.

Katherine and I could not help smiling as the ridiculous creature now scampered for the stairs, rubbing its backside, hooting, and making as much fuss as it possibly could. "You may laugh," the countess said, but without much malice. "Look what the little devil has done to my tapestry!" The monkey had pulled loose great hanks of thread.

"Does this mean that Master Summers is well again?" Katherine asked. We had heard of Master Will Summers, the king's fool and the monkey's master, but he had been sick since our arrival at court.

"Indeed he is!" said the countess, finally letting one of her giggling tiring women take the broomstick from her and brushing down her skirt.

"And he has been up here this morning with some news." She smiled, her good humour restored. "Now that he's back to normal, he's planning the masque for Christmas, and you two are to have parts."

She was right to predict that we would be delighted. Katherine, always the charmer, flew across the room to give old Malpas a spontaneous kiss on the cheek. I had to admit it was hard to resist my cousin when she was in the grip of enthusiasm.

And while I was conscious that my face had fallen into a crab-apple expression at Katherine's antics, I was thrilled too. We had heard all about the court tradition of the masque, which was to be the climax of the forthcoming twelve-day feast of Christmas. During the midwinter holiday season, troupe after troupe of players, musicians, mummers, and acrobats would be brought in to entertain us. But best of all would be the Twelfth Night masque put on by members of the court. And this year, it would also be the crowning glory of the king's wedding celebrations.

"You, Mistress Howard, are to play the part of Jealousy," Lady Malpas went on, consulting some notes on a piece of parchment, "in a rich red dress, and Mistress Camperdowne is to be Temptation, in green."

I couldn't help feeling that our roles were the wrong way round and that Katherine would have made a better Temptation. Certainly, I felt like Jealousy myself when I imagined her in a crimson satin gown. Dressed like that, she was sure to snap up the best available husband. Marriage was in the very air we breathed. Every day brought fresh speculation about what the king's new wife would be like.

"But now," the countess said, "be off with you! The king's abroad early this morning, and you should get to the Great Chamber at once." Like the monkey, we, too, rushed for the stairs, chattering as we went.

The following afternoon saw the first of our rehearsals, and these quickly became our only concern and our main topic of conversation.

When I first heard that the king had a fool, I assumed he would be a charity case like poor old Tub in Stoneton village, witless and speechless. Far from it. Will Summers, who had written the *Masque of the Vices*, as it was named, had more and better words than anyone I'd ever met.

He strode into the tennis court, which was to stand in for the Great Hall for rehearsals, looking a little like a magician, or maybe an angry bat, in his long black cloak. The white paint he wore clung to the creases of his face to turn it into a slightly sinister mask.

"Now then, my maids, mistresses, monkeys, and all," he cried, twirling around on one heel with his hand on his hip. "Tomorrow you have your costume fittings. The day after, you need to be back here to try out your chariots. Yes, each Vice will enter in a little chariot. The Master of the Revels has hired six little boys, who will come prancing out like this"— here he demonstrated a beautiful prance —"while pulling your chariots behind them. I just hope they'll be able to shift your not inconsiderable weight, ladies. Now, which Vice shall we see first? You . . . you're supposed to be Pride, are you? Well, why are you standing there drooping like Misery? Straighten up!"

I could not wait to throw myself into my part. This was my chance to make an impression upon the court.

"I think that Temptation should wriggle and writhe like this, don't you think, Master Summers?"

"She would indeed, Mistress Camperdowne, if this were a comedy," he replied, as everyone started to guffaw at my antics. "Perhaps you could aim for sultry and seductive instead of playing it for laughs. Although I do like the way you've really embraced your role."

Master Summers had even insisted that Mistress Cornwallis, who worked in the kitchens making the king's puddings, should appear in the masque as Greed. Fortunately, Mistress Cornwallis was a jolly soul and didn't mind a mockery being made of her ample girth.

Despite the general atmosphere of hilarity and lawlessness, I couldn't understand half the things that Master Summers said, and I was shocked one day when I heard him referring to the king as "Fat Face."

When I asked the Countess of Malpas why Master Summers wasn't locked up for treason, she just shrugged and said that the king's fool always had the gift of free speech, and that the king sometimes relished plain speaking after all the nonsense he got from others.

"But don't you go speaking plainly to him yourself," she warned me. "That would be dangerous."

I complained that I hardly spoke to the king at all, and that was because she herself would not let me.

"That's because you're not ready for it," she said. "Learn from your cousin Katherine. She chats to him as if he were a real human being. It's a lot of nonsense really, but he likes her compliments and flirting. Not a great lecture on the ancient history of Derbyshire like you tried to give him the other day."

Even before she had finished speaking, I opened my mouth to complain. When I'd told the royal librarian about the antiquity of Stoneton Castle, he had seemed quite fascinated, if surprised, that a maid of honour was interested in anything more than matching the colour of ribbons to dresses.

"But, Lady Malpas," I said plaintively. "I promise that I do try to listen and nod and so on."

She sighed, and for once her smile slipped from her face.

"Well, my dear," she said, "I admit that it isn't fair, but you personally have to be extra careful. Your family has a reputation for — let's say — being outspoken. And you don't want any questions about why your betrothal to the Westmorland family was broken off, do you? There is some talk that it was due to impropriety."

I stared back at her, dismayed. She was perfectly correct that it wasn't fair for people to say such things. Once more I opened my mouth to speak, but Lady Malpas raised a warning finger.

With a huge, straining effort, I just about managed to close my lips.

In the mornings, before rehearsals, we had much to prepare for the new queen's arrival. We checked off linen sheets against a huge long list, for example, and helped Lady Malpas to order supplies of soap and oil.

And we still had to be on duty in the Great Chamber when the king came forth. It had become a regular thing for both Ned and me to turn up early, well before the rest arrived. As we waited there together, we would sometimes sit on the sideboard and swing our legs in a manner that would have given the countess a fainting fit had she seen it.

And we talked.

I told Ned all about the masque rehearsal in which the Devil had accidentally got his pitchfork stuck in the wheels of my chariot. Ned revealed in return his regrets that the king, in the summer just past, had banned the rowdy but marvellous new game of football. He even leapt up to demonstrate how to play it, using his wadded-up velvet cap as the ball and placing me "in goal" in the mouth of the oriel window. Sometimes, when we were sure that no one else was around, I would flop down on one of the great floor cushions and Ned would pull me fast across the shiny boards until I shrieked with laughter.

"If only Ned were truly the son of an earl," I would sigh to myself after each of our rowdy, early morning encounters. "If only he were on the list. Of course he knows we're just friends, nothing more. Tomorrow I won't waste my time with Ned. I'll get down to the business of looking for a husband."

But somehow "tomorrow" never quite arrived.

I grew bold enough to tease Ned, mocking his habitual failure to do up his doublet properly. "I'm too busy thinking deep thoughts to bother about shallow things like *this*," he'd say, shaking the fine full sleeve of my blue dress between his fingers as if he despised it. I knew he was joking because previously — and I'd treasured the remark — he'd told me he thought it rather fetching. In order to make me giggle, he would commit increasingly ludicrous mistakes with his clothes, appearing in the Great Chamber each morning with his doublet inside out or his shoes unlaced.

And there were quieter times when we talked together in the oriel.

"I wonder if the new Queen Anne is feeling nervous," I mused one morning. "I certainly would if I had to travel across the sea to marry a strange king."

"I think it will depend on her personality," said

Ned. "Some people—your cousin Katherine, for example—might positively enjoy the challenge. But I hope that she'll be a gentle mistress to you all. The fact that it's to be a quiet wedding suggests that she might be a quiet person. Not a total strumpet like Anne Boleyn was. How the maids of honour used to complain about her!"

"Oh!" I exclaimed. Naively, I hadn't really thought before about how my life might change under the new queen. "Do you think she might be demanding and difficult? Are people ever like that with you?"

"Sometimes," Ned said, turning his cap round and round in his hands, "the senior courtiers pinch my ears or biff me round the head."

"Why would they do that?" I asked in consternation, genuinely upset for my friend.

"Well, obviously my job, as set out in the regulations, is lighting the fire," he explained, looking out of the window. "But the king uses me as a messenger. Occasionally, I have to tell people—oh, important people like the Lord Chamberlain—that the king doesn't want them coming into his private apartments that day or night."

It seemed to me to be most unfair, and I said so.

"Oh, I'm used to the unfairness," he said. "What I can't quite get used to is the idea that I'm doomed to continue lighting fires forever. I'm sure I could do something better. Something practical. I think I'd like to live on a farm."

Silence fell, but it wasn't awkward. My head was cocked in sympathy, and I sighed. It was only when Ned's face was in repose that I could see how finely shaped his cheekbones were. But I never had to wait long for his slow smile to stretch his lips once again into his characteristically wolfish grin.

"You, though," he said, "and Mistress Howard too, can certainly hope for promotion. If you make good marriages, you could become ladies-in-waiting rather than maids of honour, or even the queen's Mistress of the Robes, like the Countess of Malpas."

Talking to Ned made me realise where my career as a maid of honour might take me, which in turn made me take it more seriously. I had a guilty feeling that somehow my debut at court had fallen a little flat.

Back at Stoneton, I'd imagined myself walking

down a line of admiring courtiers, who would doff their hats and bend their legs into bows as I passed. But when I made my entrance into the Great Chamber each morning, the king's gentlemen didn't even look up and smile as they did for Katherine. Apart from Ned, most of them still seemed not to know who I was.

That's why I felt fortunate that during the period of the rehearsals, Master Summers, the king's fool, who was an important and influential person at court, somehow took to me. Gradually, I became one of his favourites.

He would often compliment me on my performance as Temptation and continued to pay me attention afterwards. When the whole court was with the king for an evening, Master Summers would address his customary entertaining commentaries on the day's events to me, pretending to assume that I would be shocked and outraged by every mundane detail of what had happened.

"Oh, my lady Carrots would be horrified to hear what my monkey said about her yesterday," he would joke. "Oh, he is quite in love with her! He pines and mourns for Mistress Temptation! Master Monkey and Mistress Temptation would make a fine pair."

For some reason I didn't mind it when he used my hated old nickname of Carrot Top or Carrots, even in front of everybody else.

One day we even met off duty, by chance in the corridor. Will Summers still had the red circles painted on his whitened cheeks for his role in the masque, and, when his face was still, the effect was aging and grotesque rather than funny.

"Hello, Carrots!" he called out jovially enough. "How are your lovers?"

I smiled and told him that, as all the world knew, I had none. "Unlike that minx the Howard girl!" he said, words that were shocking to me for I rarely heard Katherine criticised.

"Well," I said in mock reproof, "she has to beat them off with a stick."

"I cannot think why, a moody cow like her," he said casually. He must have noticed my mouth drop open at that, because he went on, "Yes, a heifer, bursting with milk, that's how I think of her.

Personally, I prefer the more astringent pleasures of Mistress Camperdowne," he added gallantly, bowing low and kissing my hand.

"Indeed!" I said. "But, kind sir, I look just like a boy!"

"A boy indeed. Or perhaps we should say an elegant elf of the woods? Certainly, there's something girlish about your green cat-eyes. But, my dear, you'll find many a courtier willing to share his bed with a beautiful boy."

I could not decide whether he'd just been appallingly rude or whether I'd just been paid the most delicious compliment of my life.

I considered the matter as I watched Master Summers's tall black figure stalking away down the corridor. He could tell that I was watching him and did the most ridiculous skip in order to make me laugh.

Perhaps, I thought to myself, I should not content myself with always being guided by, and measuring myself against, Katherine.

Perhaps I should dare to be a little different.

Chapter 19

The New Queen

6 JANUARY 1540

At very long last, the morning of the king's marriage to Anne of Cleves arrived. And, almost even more exciting, in its wake would come the night of the masque. We were mad with impatience for both events to begin.

As we went off towards the royal rooms, Katherine was in one of her ebullient moods and poked me in the ribs. "Look at us now, hey, Carrots?" she said. "Off to hobnob with the queen. Wouldn't the girls at Trumpton be jealous?"

I couldn't help but smile back, and we strutted

along in our coloured gowns, conscious that we made an attractive pair.

Our spirits fell a little as we passed through the door into the hush of the royal suite. The queen's apartments had been shut up since the death of Queen Jane, and our way was illuminated by shafts of weak sunlight penetrating through windows still only half unshuttered. We came to the threshold of the queen's private closet, a place in the palace we had never previously been allowed to enter.

Our new mistress had come to Greenwich some days before, but since then she had been closeted away with her own German attendants. So we were wild to know what manner of a woman she was. The king's fourth marriage was to be kept strictly private. I think after the great public show he'd made of his earlier marriages, and with their very public failure, he felt safer behind closed doors. But now, the wedding ceremony was complete, and Katherine and I were called into the closet to make our curtseys.

The sight of the two of them still standing side by side in front of the priest, not speaking, not touching, recalled my own experience, so many years ago, when I had "married" Sir Dudley. It was not a pleasant memory. I knew perfectly well that, despite what the minstrels said, marriage need not involve love.

I shuddered. One day I, too, would have to stand there like that, hoping and praying the man I had just married would turn out to be a good husband.

I knew that the new queen was twenty-four years old, but was astonished now to observe how much younger than that she looked. Perhaps this was partly by contrast to her husband. It would be treason to dare to speak the words, but the king appeared rather older than his forty-eight years, with his stick, his belly, and his bad foot.

Katherine and I by now both knew the king well enough to realise that he was in a bad temper. We exchanged glances.

"Ah, here are your maids," he grunted as he saw us, giving us a dismissive nod. "Her Majesty is not well. Help her away."

To our surprise, the new queen came forward, rather than waiting for us to approach her, and took us each by the hand. I noticed that her hand in mine was shaking, and I saw that her face, beneath her foreign-looking white hood, was even whiter. She was blinking back tears. Gradually, supporting her, we shuffled out of the room.

We went to the queen's own chamber, and there it was shocking to find that Queen Anne seemed rather like a convent girl. Although she was older than us, I guessed that she knew even less about the world than we did. She could hardly speak English, as we had been warned, but no one had told us that she would also dress so oddly, like a nun.

Queen Anne went almost immediately to lie on her bed and turned to face the wall. Katherine and I, at a loss for something to do, looked through her dresses to choose one suitable for her to wear to the masque. But they all seemed to be black or dark coloured, and it was sorry work.

As the daylight faded, we managed to coax her off her bed and into the finest gown that we could find. Despite our efforts, the queen fairly failed to open her mouth to speak at all that afternoon. And she smiled only when the German *Fräuleins* she had brought with her from home came in to give her their congratulations on her marriage.

I'm not at all sure what the new queen made of our masque that evening. It started late, and despite our rehearsals, every scene hopelessly overran in terms of timing. By the time we Vices were ready to make our entry in our chariots, the spectators had all been drinking wine for hours. We could hear shouts and jeers as we waited in the backstage area, nervous and impatient at the same time. Again and again I resettled my sleeveless green satin toga upon my shoulder, as it had a tendency to slip down. But I could hardly suppress my smile when Ned Barsby slipped out into the passage where we waited to wish us luck. He was wearing Master Summers's jester's cap and looked a little harassed.

"Be prepared for a bit of action," he warned us. "They're not in the mood for art appreciation."

"Oh, Lord!" said Katherine. "Will we be safe?"

I was pleased that Ned ignored her fussing and instead helped me into my chariot.

"Lovely dress!" he said quietly, dipping his head so that the bells on his cap jingled against my cheek. "It's wasted on these barbarians." His hand was grasping the green-painted bar around the front of my chariot. I had a sudden certainty that if I placed my own hand nearby, his hand would touch mine as if by accident. As if Ned had the same thought at the same time, our fingers made contact in midair. I gasped. It was as if lightning momentarily flashed between us, as if I really were the powerful goddess Temptation.

Calm down! I told myself. *It's only Ned. No one important.*

But Will Summers was hissing at Ned to get out of the way, and our chariots jolted into motion. I felt a rosy glow rising to my cheeks as I turned my head back towards Ned to say goodbye. This meant that I entered the Great Hall looking the wrong way, and all of our carefully rehearsed choreography was wiped from my mind.

Ned was wise to have warned us about the state of the court. As I turned round to face the audience, the gentlemen courtiers fairly hollered and slavered over us maids of honour. "I feel the Vice of Lust!" yelled one of them, seeing our costumes. "Begone, Vice!" shouted another, and he and the rest of them began to pelt us with sugar plums and the occasional hard and hurtful nut.

It was a struggle to smile, but glancing round at Katherine, I saw her beatific beam in place as usual and her arm curved high above her head in an attitude of wonderful grace. The dance! I had forgotten! I frantically tried to remember which limb I was supposed to raise and attempted to look as if I, too, were enjoying myself.

During the banquet that followed, the queen sat silently at the top table, clearly trying hard to look relaxed, while the king openly neglected her, twisting round in his chair to talk to other people. I felt chagrined on her part and crept up behind her to whisper in her ear that she should signal if she wanted anything.

"Cunning little devil to curry favour like that!" Katherine hissed, as I returned to my place. But in all honesty I had merely guessed that Queen Anne did not know our customs and might have been sitting there in need of the close-stool or a handkerchief without quite knowing how to ask for it.

In our bed late that night, though, the January moon peeping in through the window, my final thought was not of the wedding day of the queen or the disappointment the long-awaited masque had brought. It was of Ned's hand meeting mine midair. I wondered if he was sleeping or, like me, looking at the moon. I recalled the moment our hands had touched again and again, time after time, until sleep lowered my lids.

Chapter 20

No Blood

7 JANUARY 1540

The next morning we were all tired after the late night, but the Countess of Malpas and the other married ladies-in-waiting were up early and eagerly. It was their duty to strip the queen's bed, carefully searching for evidence that the king had taken his pleasure there in the night. Katherine and I, as unmarried maids, were not permitted to be present. But the news of the investigation's result flashed around the whole palace just as fast as a bout of contagious sweating sickness. It was Will Summers who came to our chamber to tell us, hardly waiting for an answer to his knock before charging in through the door.

"No blood," he said shortly, before turning smartly round and leaving.

We knew at once what he meant, and Katherine audibly sucked her breath through her teeth. The ladies-in-waiting had found no blood or other substances on the sheets, no trace of proof that the king and new queen had consummated their marriage, no hint that an heir was on the way. I presumed that Will had rushed off to spread the gossip even further and gain as much credit as he could by being first with the news.

"Silly German sow!" Katherine said as soon as the door had swung shut. "If I were her, I wouldn't go round with that gaggle of German nuns in tow. I'd consult the best astrologers about the time to conceive and ask the best midwife for advice, and I'd get on with it."

"Children are God's gift, Katherine," I said, perhaps somewhat primly. I, too, felt intense curiosity about what might or might not have happened, but I also felt it was unseemly to show it. "They may come or they may not."

"Oh, that's all right for you and Master Summers and the intellectuals to say," Katherine said, tossing back her head and inspecting her nails. "Remember Queen Katherine of Aragon. People say the king had to divorce her because she couldn't get pigged up again after Princess Mary. Remember Queen Anne Boleyn. Her piglets were all either dead or female. And look what happened to her. Fools, both of them."

She gave an evil snigger. "There are ways to make it happen."

I turned away, unwilling to share her smugness. "But what do you mean 'me and Master Summers,' anyway?" I asked as an afterthought.

"Ha!" said Katherine. "Everyone knows that he likes boys who look like girls and girls who look like boys." Again she had me speechless. I leaned back in my chair and tried hard to look blasé rather than reply.

"I prefer a good red-blooded man myself," she went on. "And I don't mean Ned," she added, with a warning jab of her finger. "It's beyond me why you waste your time on him. Can't you see that you'll never hook an earl or a baron while you have a base-born page buzzing round? I'm off to see if old Malpas has any more lurid details."

The door banged. Alone in the room after being abandoned for the second time in two minutes, I jumped up and paced about. I felt intensely angry with my know-it-all cousin for being so worldly and cruel.

And, while I was reluctant to admit it, I was angry with myself too. Successful maids of honour, I told myself as I chewed viciously upon a sliver of finger-nail, were supposed to be besieged by gallants. Just like Katherine was.

I had to try harder. The only two admirers I had were a humble bastard-born page and a man who didn't like women.

Chapter 21

Caught

JANUARY 1540

Darkness had fallen hours ago, and the gleaming tiles of the palace cloister were icy beneath my slippers. At intervals, the glowing coals of the braziers illuminated the watchful faces of the guards. Yet the tall Yeomen of the Guard waved us through doorway after doorway. For once I was among the chosen few, expected and welcomed. It felt good.

A few days after the marriage and the masque, I was enjoying the chance to pay a visit of my own to the very heart of all the controversy: the queen's bedchamber.

The Countess of Malpas had asked for my assistance in undressing our mistress. I scurried along a respectful half pace behind her. It was always a bit of a struggle to keep up with the countess. She could move her little legs so fast and yet so smoothly that it looked as if she ran on wheels.

"I commend you, Mistress Camperdowne," she said over her shoulder as we went along, "for your attentiveness to the queen. It has not gone unnoticed."

And so I glowed a little with self-satisfaction as we entered the queen's fire-lit bedchamber and made our curtseys. I had indeed held myself apart from the courtiers who joked about the queen's strange German headgear and her guttural voice when she tried to speak English.

We were to prepare our mistress for bed, and the countess began to unlace the stiff carapace of the queen's gown. She always wore black and other dark colours, despite her young age, finely made of course but oddly sombre. The unlacing took quite some time. As usual with the taciturn Queen Anne, silence fell.

"Madam, we hope you may soon be bringing the

English court a son!" said the countess brightly and with what sounded to me like rather a desperate lunge at a topic for conversation.

"Ach, so says the king," she replied, looking down at her hands as she sat patiently, the countess unstitching her back. It was like the shedding of the skin of a caterpillar, and fine billows of the queen's voluminous white shift came gradually into view as the countess's hands worked.

"Well, he comes to you every night to do the work of a husband, does he not?" the countess said, in an encouraging tone.

Now Anne looked up with a little smile. Only when she gave her rare and gentle smile did her face remind me of the image Master Holbein had made. There had been great scandal whispered round the court at the trick his picture had played upon us all, for truly the queen was not beautiful. Or maybe we thought this because we only ever saw her frowning or glum.

"Indeed!" she said with a quiet air of triumph. "Every night he come, he kiss me, he say 'Good night, sweetheart,' and he sleep just here!" She nodded at the enormous carved bed in the centre of the room.

"Your Majesty, there must be more done than that if you are to bring us a boy!" said the countess, in a voice that sounded slightly shocked. I looked quickly down at the linen night shift I held in my hands, hardly knowing where to direct my eyes in the face of this revelation.

I sensed rather than saw the countess give me the sternest of warning glances, a look that clearly spelled out that she would kill me if I told anyone that our queen was obviously ignorant of the facts of life.

"Off with you, Mistress Eliza," she said. "I can finish alone."

"Good night, Your Majesty." I bobbed my curtsey and placed the folded shift on the bed. Just outside the door, I could not resist lingering for an instant. With horrified delight, I realised that back in the royal bedchamber the countess must be explaining to the queen, a grown woman and the mistress of us all, exactly how babies were made.

And so I was caught.

As I lingered outside the door, my hand still touching it and my head still turning from side to side in wonder, a pair of hands suddenly grasped my waist from behind.

I yelped. But the hands were strong and it was a man's breath that was blowing hot, winey, and intimidating into my ear. By now I knew enough of palace life to understand that some predators are best beaten off with discretion and the minimum of noise, so I tensed myself to swing round with a vicious kick rather than a scream. But then I realised I could do neither.

"Well, my little elf!"

It was the king, of course, come early to the queen's bedchamber for the night. I froze, my arms and legs completely transformed into ice. I dared not turn to face him, and he seemed quite content to press himself against my behind, in turn pressing me against the jamb of the door. In a moment my cheek was crushed against its wood.

"My wife's maid a-listening at the door, eh?" he whispered. "You won't hear much to heat your blood in there," he muttered as if to himself. "You maids of honour are a scurrilous lot, I know," he added, breathing into my ear again more insistently and actually nudging it with his horrid wet lips. "You need to give her a lesson or two!" I felt a hot hand briefly clamp itself to my bottom, before he pushed me out of the way and opened his wife's chamber door.

Shaken and revolted, I slipped away with an urgent desire to return to my own room. I consoled myself with the thought that at least my royal pawing hadn't been witnessed.

After three months at the court, I should have known better.

I would later learn that someone, somewhere in the shadows, had been watching. In a royal palace every wall has ears, and eyes are hidden behind each twist of the corridor. My encounter with the king had not been unobserved.

Chapter 22

It's a Secret We Have to Keep

L ate that night I crept into our bed and lay there silently whimpering until I could bear it no longer, and I had to let my sobs shake the bedframe.

"Eliza! What is it? Is it Ned?"

Katherine, bleary-eyed with interrupted sleep, was up on one elbow, lighting the candle and looking at me with genuine concern.

"Katherine," I said uncertainly. I hated to reveal a weakness to her, but I had a burning need to know. "How can you bear it when the gentlemen of the court leer at us? They don't mean it either, when they give us those chivalrous compliments. They're just laughing at us and talking behind our backs about which of us they'd most like to have in bed."

"Oh, men!" Katherine flumped back on the pillows, rubbing the heels of her hands into her eyes. "It's always men, isn't it? They're just children really. Whatever man's been horrid to you, Eliza, you should imagine him as he once was, crawling round on the floor, bawling for his nurse and pooing his linen. You have to grow up, Eliza, take it in your stride."

But I could not seem to take it in my stride. I had come to court to find a husband to whom I would be joined in legal, holy matrimony. My father had sent me here for this purpose, surely. I did not understand how Katherine could be so relaxed. And I could hardly credit that the king himself had pushed me up against a door, like any common doxy of the streets. It seemed to me to be more than just wrong; it seemed actually to be wicked.

But of this I dared not speak, and Katherine did not press me. Soon her breathing evened out once more, but I went on staring at the candle flame until it guttered out in a pool of wax.

***

I kept my secret to myself for several dismal and lonely weeks. In March, when the roads became passable, I began to look forward to my father and my aunt arriving at Greenwich for a long-planned visit. Heavy rain and floods delayed them, though, which disappointed me, for I was quite longing to see them again.

In fact, my father and aunt arrived quite unexpectedly one evening, when Katherine, I, and other ladies were performing the "Dance of the Nine Muses" in the Great Chamber after dinner, for the amusement of the king and his cronies.

We were old hands at this dance now, able to dip low and reach high so easily that we had leisure to bestow Katherine's "killing" glances upon members of the audience if we so chose. At one point I caught Ned's glance, and we exchanged a comic grimace, as if the whole thing was a joke. But, almost unwillingly, my body began to perform more gracefully in the knowledge that he was watching.

It was halfway through the performance that I spotted the two new arrivals being led into the room by two gentleman ushers. I would have recognised them anywhere, and I was so glad to see my relations that I composed myself with some difficulty to see the dance through to its conclusion.

The king, too, had noticed the newcomers. "Lord Stone!" he shouted out genially, gesturing at me with his goblet. "How do you like your daughter now that she belongs to me?" Blushing, I bowed my head to my father. I saw that he was a little bewildered at being yelled at without having even yet made his formal bow, but that he was also smiling with undisguised pleasure.

"Your Majesty," he said, "I see that under your care she has become a woman."

And indeed I had, I thought, as I straightened up to my full height then bent down to my lowest. I had grown up more than he could have possibly suspected.

I went over to curtsey to my father, and then rose up again to receive his kiss. I had something of a shock when I raised my head and saw him close up in the light of the chamber's many candelabra. His little beard was now almost entirely white, and he seemed very thin and rheumy around the eyes.

"Father, how is Stoneton?" I asked. "Is everybody well? Did Mr. Nutkin survive the winter?"

He smiled and nodded, then turned, rather child-like, to Aunt Margaret, who repeated what I'd said.

"Speak louder, into his left ear," she suggested. It was blissful to see their familiar faces again after so long and wonderful to introduce them to my colleagues at the court. But something of their colour seemed to have faded.

Later, I persuaded Katherine to go and sleep with another maid of honour in order to make room in our bed for my aunt Margaret. When the curtains were closed and our little den was illuminated with just one candle, it was very cosy indeed.

"So, Eliza," she said, twisting her grey hair into a bunch for sleeping, "what is it really like at court? Are you having as much fun as it seems?"

"Well . . ."

I wanted Aunt Margaret to think that I was always as graceful and as poised as she had seen me in the middle of the dance. But I found it hard to meet her searching, bright, bird-like gaze. I bent to pull off my sheepskin slippers and drop them to the floor.

"Eliza!"

There was no getting away from it. She wanted the whole story.

"Well . . ." I began again.

"I think, Eliza," Aunt Margaret said, looking up at the bed canopy, "you must have learned a hard lesson or two while you've been here. Everyone in England looks up to King Henry the Eighth, don't they, accepting that he is appointed by God and that he can do no wrong? But the reality is a little different, isn't it?"

I could hardly credit that my aunt, my strait-laced, upright aunt, was verging upon treason in her conversation. Of course we had been taught exactly what she said, from our very cradles, and our early belief in the king's virtue, kindness, justice, and mercy was reinforced by every priest and teacher and lord in the land.

At court, though, it was immediately obvious that this was not true. We could not ignore the evidence of our eyes that the king, God's anointed chosen monarch, was in fact a gluttonous, predatory old man.

"It's as if it's a secret we have to keep from the rest of the world," I said in a rush. I whispered, so nervous I was of putting this thought into words. I even tweaked open the bed curtains and scanned the shadows of the room beyond to make sure we were really alone. "It's as if all of us courtiers are in on the secret, and it creates a bond between us. The king is sometimes stupid and greedy and wrong."

"That's my girl." Aunt Margaret rolled on her side to look at me. "I was at court too, you know, long ago."

I had forgotten this and looked at her with renewed interest. Aunt Margaret? Dressing up, dancing, performing in masques?

"And that's how I know it's a poisonous swamp, the palace. Danger everywhere. You know certain things, but you have to act as if you don't. You must remember, Eliza, that while you may not admire every single action of the king's, he holds the power of life or death in his hands. *Your* life or death. You can never, never let on what you know."

I nodded. But I felt a whirring in my brain, like a clock being wound up. I had never thought of my aunt as a courtier like me. Come to think of it, I had never thought of her as young like me. I decided to take advantage of the hour and the atmosphere of confidence to ask what had really been happening at Stoneton.

"Things are bad," she admitted. "Your father has never been any good at managing the estate, of course, and we have had to sell more land." I pursed my lips as did my aunt herself upon hearing bad tidings. Obviously, her words made me uneasy, but I also felt a glow of pride that she was now treating me to adult news and views.

But then an awful thought struck me. Would she ask me outright if I was likely to receive any proposals of marriage soon? That was our one hope for saving the estate. How could I say that I'd made no progress at all? I tensed myself in readiness.

"Still," she said, surprising me with her warmth, "you are obviously prospering here. The king has not been so welcoming to us since the events of . . . well, before."

My shoulders relaxed. So I was safe! I decided to press my advantage home to learn something I'd always been curious about. "What happened to my uncle, Aunt Margaret?"

I knew it was something dreadful—I had seen it in the reactions of certain courtiers when they heard my name for the first time. "I know that we had to pay the 'Great Forfeit,' but I don't know what it was for."

"For treason, child," said my aunt in a resigned voice. "My elder brother was engaged to . . . a certain lady. I won't tell you her name. It's ancient history now. The king took a fancy to the same lady and insisted that she go to his bed. My brother was furious, and, despite everything I said, he wouldn't keep quiet. He insisted that the ancient family of Camperdowne deserved better. The king didn't even get angry. He just waved a hand, and my brother was taken to the Tower of London. There he refused to back down, silly fool, and eventually he was executed."

I shuddered and twitched up the fur coverlet about my shoulders.

"That's why pride, my dear, is dangerous as well as sinful, as I have told you all your life," my aunt went on. "You just can't afford to think that you know better than the king, or that the rules don't apply to you. The fine we had to pay nearly ruined us and depleted the Camperdowne lands. . . . I can't tell you how much we grieved and lamented his foolish pride."

Aunt Margaret's fist was moving up and down, almost as if it still held her cane and she were banging it on the floor to emphasise her words.

"And that's why you, Eliza," she continued, "and your marriage are so important to the future of the family. But, to be completely honest, your father and I have been struggling to find a family who will ally with us since we were tainted." She had somehow got herself into a sitting position once again during the course of her lecture.

"There was only the Earl of Westmorland, who counted on our being so out of the swing of things at Stoneton that we would not know about the bad character of his son. So much rides on your making a success of yourself here at the court."

With that Aunt Margaret pinched my cheek, pinched out the candle, reached down to put the holder on the floor, and lay down to sleep. I stayed awake for a long time, looking up into the dark. My mind wanted to dwell upon Ned's eyes, his hands, his lips.

But I batted the thought away.

Aunt Margaret had just reminded me that I could not afford it. I had kept my distance from Ned recently, doubly so since Katherine had warned me that spending time with him would damage my prospects. Yet I still felt his eyes upon me as we trod the same floorboards each day in the Great Chamber, at chapel, and at the feast.

I forced myself to think instead about my unknown uncle. How had he managed to muddle things up so badly? I knew that my uncle was not the first to fall foul of the king, and I feared that he would not be the last.

Just before sleep came, I looked over at my aunt's face on the pillow, its deep lines visible even in the gentle glow of starlight that crept through a crack in the bed curtains. Could it be that she had changed, grown softer and weaker, since I had seen her last? Even her cane now seemed to be something she needed for walking rather than just a prop for bossiness. Or perhaps the change was in me.

Chapter 23

The King's Mistress

MARCH 1540

My father and I were shuffling slowly along the broad walk by the wide grey river, heavily wrapped in our furred cloaks. It was freezing cold, but his step was uncertain, and he would not be hurried. This was the day after his and Aunt Margaret's arrival at Greenwich, and the first time we had been alone.

"I understand," he said, "you have done very well for yourself here at the court. Henny says you have become a great lady indeed."

I was pleased by his words, but a slender sliver of doubt pricked me in the stomach. I suspected that

Henny thought I had become too fine a lady in some of my ways. I circled my arms vigorously a couple of times, and not just because of the cold. Perhaps it was babyish of me to worry about pleasing my old nurse.

The riverbank was enlivened by the occasional cargo ship on its way up to the port of London. It was a good place to talk. The open ground meant we could see that no one was in earshot, and my father spoke rather loudly now to compensate for his loss of hearing.

"And Aunt Margaret tells me you have been giving some further thought to the matter of my marriage?" I asked him, slipping my hand through the crook of the arm left free from his stick.

Even as I did so, my unruly imagination insisted on reminding me how my heart would swell should Ned suddenly step into sight on the path before us. I shook my head to clear it and get back to business.

There was a long pause, while my father looked out across the water. The sharp wind had made his eyes run slightly.

"Indeed," he said, and sighed. "To be frank," he

continued a little impatiently, "the matter does not go prettily. As you are such a woman of the world now, I can speak openly."

He sighed again and twitched his head towards me in his old fox-like manner.

"There is the matter of our unfortunate brother that goes against our family," he said drily. "Then there was the matter of the Viscount Westmorland. Although you really were blameless, there was some scandalous talk about the affair."

Another pause followed, and a glum silence descended over us both. I bowed my head and looked at the path. I had so looked forward to seeing him again and had hoped for better news than this.

"Rosebud," he finally said, slowing his pace still further and reaching for my hand. He fumbled a little in his heavy gloves. "Marriage need not be the only solution to our problems, you know. There are other ways to win riches at court."

"What in God's name do you mean?" I cried, drawing him to a halt in the middle of the pathway and trying to withdraw my hand from his. I had a horrible premonition of what his answer might be.

"Well, I have heard that the king has taken a great interest in you," he said, as if unwillingly. "A great *personal* interest in you, I mean."

So someone *had* seen the king squeezing me tightly in his arms! I knew that gossip flew constantly round the palace, but the Countess of Malpas had warned me plainly enough that I must never feature in it. I could feel my cheeks grow red. Would my father despise me for being bold and saucy — as he had done once before when I met the viscount?

But he had more to say and said it while looking right past me, fixing his glassy stare on the choppy waves.

"Through all the years of history," he continued, "the king has always taken a mistress, you know, as well as a wife. The mistress is well rewarded, with riches and with influence as well. As you know, the king needs children. Even illegitimate children are better than no children. If the king should ever ask you to share his bed —"

This was not at all what I had expected. "Father!" I cried out.

"You should not say no."

I could hardly bear to stay with him and listen to this, for it seemed such a betrayal. But neither could I leave this old man out here all alone with his stick.

He sighed again, patting my hand gently between both of his clumsy gloved paws. Now he looked into my eyes, and I looked back to see the water from his eyes was brimming over on to his cheeks.

"It would be a great gift to our family, Rosebud," he said, "if you were to become the king's mistress."

Chapter 24

I Cannot Tell You What to Do

As I hurried back to my chamber, both arms hugging my furry cloak close to my body, I had never before felt in such need of a friend.

My own father, suggesting this! Matters at Stoneton must have grown desperate indeed for him to recommend such a course, I thought, as I trudged from the garden into the cloister without really seeing either.

But a sudden thought brought me to a complete stand still, and a passing page boy almost bumped into me.

I'd remembered that my father had already tried to marry me off to a drunken and inconstant lout. Perhaps — astonishing thought — his judgement was flawed? Or perhaps I was being naive, and everyone would think me a fool if I were to turn down such an offer from the king . . . should it ever be made.

But to whom could I talk for advice? I pondered the matter as I quickly changed my dress to go on duty. Certainly not to Katherine nor the Countess of Malpas. Nor even Henny, who was now doing my bodice up at the back with her customary efficiency. No, it would have to be someone who knew both me and the wicked world of the court. And it would have to be someone whom I could trust with my life.

"Ned!" I hissed sharply, as he passed my station in front of the elephant tapestry, carrying his bundle of faggots towards the fireplace. He pretended to drop a piece of wood, scrabbling on the floor to rearrange his load and secretly smiling up at me through his silky fringe. He had his shirtsleeves rolled up a little, reminding me that he did real work, unlike the foppish middle-aged courtiers who fawned round the king. We both glanced at the king's party, busy at cards at the other end of the Great Chamber near the warmth of the fireplace. They were happily engaged in their game, paying us no heed. "Meet me in the banqueting house at four!" I whispered, as discreetly as I could.

The deep chimes of the palace clock kept us all to our schedules, but today they seemed to take their time in coming. But I knew that Ned would not let me down unless the king himself had demanded some whim be met. Once more wrapped in my warmest cloak, I scurried through the darkening garden to the little turreted building that the king used on summer evenings for listening to music. I knew too that Ned would somehow have got hold of its key, even though it was supposed to be locked up and out of bounds at this time of year. He had excellent contacts. Ned could obtain any key to any door, however private.

I was right — the stiff, cobwebby door creaked open at my shove. The banqueting house was cold, of course, and a melancholy scatter of mouse droppings trailed across its floor. The blank eyes of ancient goddesses and nymphs gazed from the painted walls and ceilings. But Ned was there, bouncing up like a puppy and smiling in welcome. His teeth were so white that I could see his grin floating in the darkness. He had with him a little horn lantern, dark on three sides, casting just enough light to see, but not enough to arouse suspicion.

He quickly sat me down on a cushionless bench, laying his own cloak across my knees. Ned laughed at my protests, telling me that he never felt the cold. "Now then, are you ready to see my marvellous new trick?" he asked, whipping out his tinderbox. His job had made him a master of fire-lighting, and he had so many different ways of striking sparks from his flint that I often teased him for being obsessed.

"No, Ned!" I spoke more sharply than I'd meant to. "Not now. Something's happened."

Instantly, he was all ears, and his arm was round my shoulders. I luxuriated for a moment in its warmth and weight. It was very difficult to begin, and I could not meet his eyes, but I explained everything that my father had said. When I had finished, I sat quietly, hanging my head a little, but feeling more peaceful inside for having let it all out.

But Ned's arm had dropped away, and he turned from me on the bench. He seemed strangely troubled by my story, so much so that a worm of worry started to writhe in my stomach again, even more violently than before. "This is not so unusual, is it?" I begged him. "Surely you have heard a tale like this before?"

"Yes," he said somewhat distantly. "It's true that everyone said the lady Anne was the king's mistress while Queen Katherine was still the queen, and then the future Queen Jane was seen sitting on the king's knee while Queen Anne still lived. It has happened before."

"Well, then," I said. I began to wonder if he thought I had been presumptuous in supposing that the king could possibly find me attractive. Perhaps it was my ridiculous pride, once again, that had simply been setting me up for a fall.

"I know that I'm not plump or fertile or beautiful," I said. "I'm sorry to have wasted your time, Ned.

I don't know how I could have thought that the king would ever seriously want me."

"Oh, come on!" Ned sounded almost annoyed. "You know better than that. You're as bad as the rest of the bloody maids of honour, fishing for compliments. You must know that all the gentlemen of the court exchange huge sums of money just betting on the colour of the stockings you wear each day on your long legs."

This at least had the effect of jolting me out of my misery.

"But how do they know?" I asked in some bewilderment. "I am very decorous and never lift my skirt. I don't go in for all that French toe-pointing like some of the maids do."

"That's true. You always keep your legs together, unlike Mistress Howard. I think that hoity-toity French tiring woman of Mistress Howard's finds out what you're wearing underneath," he said vaguely, as if not really interested. "She probably asks Henny and sells the information. Hoity-toity she may be, but she's not too grand to take a bribe."

"Why don't I know anything about this?"

"Because the gentlemen are frightened of you. You're cleverer than they are. You laugh at them, and it hurts them. That's why they're all attracted to the idea of bending you to their will." This was a new concept to me. I began to turn it slowly over in my mind, considering it from all angles. I got up suddenly from the bench in order to disperse a fresh cloud of unpleasant ideas. Ned's voice once again interrupted my train of thought.

"But you — you, Eliza, as the king's mistress!"

The words burst from him, as if against his will. He grabbed my hand, pulled me back down towards the seat, and looked urgently into my eyes. Although I had studied them so often, I felt that I had never noticed before just how shapely his eyebrows were. Then he dropped my hand and turned away once again.

"I hoped that you wanted something else. Something . . . different, not this. Nothing like this at all. I cannot tell you what to do."

With that he jumped up, took away his lantern and his light, and began barring up the shutters of the window.

Our conversation was so strange and unsatisfactory that it had made me feel worse, far worse. I stared at him in consternation. What did he mean by "something . . . different"? Surely he didn't mean me and him, together? Surely he *couldn't* mean me and him?

Ned was still in the room with me, dropping the shutter bars into place with needless force, but I felt terribly alone. I stood up abruptly.

Without another word, I walked out and banged the heavy door.

Chapter 25

Choice

I trudged back through the gardens, leaving Ned to finish the locking up. My hands were freezing even inside my cloak. An icy little wind had started up, and the iron weather vanes set in the centre of each small square flower bed were beginning to turn and whistle.

"I thought you were supposed to be my *friend*, Ned," I muttered to myself. "I wanted advice from you, not mysterious riddles."

I wished that I'd had the wit to say it earlier, when I was still with him.

"I'd better just keep away from you, Ned, if I make you feel bad," I declared, with melodramatic passion. "It's not as if we could ever marry. I really hope you didn't mean that."

Then it occurred to me that if anyone could see me strolling in the wintry garden after dark, talking to myself, they'd assume I'd gone crazy.

The palace lights, twinkling blurrily behind latticed panes, seemed warm and inviting, and I felt the urge for something to thaw me out. Unusually, I decided to go to the buttery adjoining the Great Hall and ask for a glass of spiced wine. We all had this privilege, though we maids of honour rarely used it. We preferred to eat in the Great Chamber, or else to have our servants bring us food and drink in our comfortable rooms rather than share the common benches with the lower servants. Indeed, I had not sat with the general run of the household staff since the very first night of our arrival, when Katherine and I had known no better.

Of course I had been expecting far too much when I'd had the idea of spiced wine. They didn't have anything so fancy at the buttery bar. I hadn't the energy to refuse the proffered alternative of ale. I took my cup through to the hall and sat gloomily by myself at one of the long tables, empty at that time of day apart from the usual huddle of young men talking about the Lord knows what nasty business in the corner. I felt I couldn't bear for one of my colleagues from the state apartments to have seen me at that moment, and that at least here no one would know who I was.

After a moment, though, I realised that I was under surveillance. I was surprised to see Will Summers detach himself from the noisy group of stable lads and bakers' assistants, and come towards me with his snake-hipped walk.

"All alone, my lover?" he said, sitting down companionably beside me. "This isn't quite the place for a maid of honour to be, you know."

"Of course not," I said, hoping that I didn't look as grumpy as I felt. "But I just wanted to be left alone for a while, and not be with the great gaggle of girls upstairs."

"Pondering our future, are we?" he asked, not unkindly. "I hear it speculated that great things are in store for you, indeed that the king himself has his eye upon your pert behind."

"Indeed, and a great burden to me the matter has become!" I burst out. It was surely indiscreet and dangerous, but I knew that Will Summers was wily and wise. I needed someone, at least, to be on my side. I noticed that in a normal doublet and hose, not his usual curious multicoloured costume, he looked handsome and almost like a fine young lord. For a moment I wished that he was indeed a lord and that my father could contract me in marriage to him. In a partnership with Will I suspected that there would be kindness, tolerance, and humour.

"Now, Eliza," he said sternly. "I can see what's going on."

"Oh, is that so, Master Summers?" I said sharply, banging down my pewter cup on the table. I was further distressed at the notion my private affairs were so transparent. "Do give me the benefit of your advice."

"It's simple," he said, calmly pushing my cup out of his way and leaning on the table towards me. "And it's clear what you should do. Don't throw away your chances through some fine feelings about your honour. One of the most powerful positions at court is vacant at the moment. The king needs a mistress, it's clear. He's not getting what he wants from his wife. And a mistress has an untold opportunity for getting what she wants — or, if not what she herself wants, what her friends want."

I could see that he was earnestly giving me what he believed to be good counsel.

"But, Will — *would you?*"

"I know what you mean. That ulcer gives off a hideous stench. I have to put up with it myself when I entertain the king as the doctor gives his leg its mineral bath." He laughed, but it was an uneasy sound.

"But think of it this way, Carrots," he began again. "One day you will have to marry — you won't have any choice — and your husband will inevitably not be to your taste either. There's no fairy-tale prince waiting to whisk you away to a life of romance, my dear. Master Barsby isn't for the likes of you."

I winced, but Will ignored me.

"Your business in life," he said, "will be solely to bear some unattractive man his snotty children . . . unless you choose to do something about it. You're clever enough to understand what I'm saying."

I thought hard.

I had decided to cut Ned right out of my thoughts; he was too difficult, too upsetting. That much was clear. And certainly it could feel good to take action, to settle upon a future for myself.

The idea started to grow on me. It was a challenge. I could see that many things I desired — jewels and influence — might be mine for the taking. In fact, why in heaven not? Why not make my own choice? I had never dreamed I had such power. . . .

What about making a fresh start on my court career, with no thoughts of Ned to hold me back and glittering treasures ahead of me?

I suddenly looked up and saw that Will was still watching me, smiling a little. I felt a blush rising up across my cheeks. I feared that he had been able to read my whole succession of thoughts as they had crossed my face.

"Thank you kindly, Master Summers," I said, draining my goblet and standing up decisively. "That is indeed a most interesting idea."

Chapter 26

Queen No More

SUMMER 1540

It was an interesting thought, but I did not act upon it straightaway, not least because I liked and respected my own mistress, Queen Anne.

The king did not pick me out again for attention as spring slipped into summer, and I kept well away from Ned Barsby too. He was hardly ever in the Great Chamber. It was only by accident that I discovered where he had got to.

"What's that? Were you asking why we never see Master Barsby?" The Countess of Malpas was speaking to another of the maids of honour, but I overheard her words. "I believe that he has requested a transfer to serve in the private dining chamber, instead of with us in the Great Chamber." Without Ned to joke about with, the long evenings sometimes seemed endlessly dull. But I told myself that his transfer was the best thing for us both.

I continued to wait upon the poor neglected queen, and when we were together in her own apartments, we often had gay times, laughing and joking. Gradually, we managed to get her into more becoming clothes, and even induced her to start drinking wine.

And yet there was a sense of doom about the whole enterprise of her being queen. There was clearly no sign of a pregnancy, and the king gave up coming to her chambers at night. Katherine was also less and less assiduous in her attendance. In fact, it was almost as though she had ceased to be a maid of honour, and I was not sure how she was spending her time instead.

The Countess of Malpas gave us dreadful warnings against gossiping about the king and queen's relationship — or the lack of it. "We do not discuss the king's private relationship, even among ourselves," she said, as stern as I had ever seen her. "He has placed his trust in our mistress the queen. He believes that God will give her a baby boy, so we must do that too."

Will Summers told me that he and all the gentlemen had been called to a special meeting to hear the results of an enquiry by the royal doctors into the king's health.

"His Majesty is well able 'to do the act' with any woman he should choose," Will hissed into my ear as he partnered me into chapel. "We heard it straight from the mouth of all three royal doctors. Just not with his wife. She's simply too unattractive."

Katherine had made a rare appearance in the chapel, and I was pleased to see her scowling at us from across the aisle, aware that she was missing out on Will's well-informed gossip.

This news about the king's virility was one of many things that half of me would have liked to talk over with Ned. Yet whenever I saw him in the courtyard or cloisters, I simply dipped my head and went on walking. I sometimes caught myself listening for his name on the lips of my colleagues as they talked over all the news of the palace.

I schooled myself when I heard it to produce a

weary sneer. "Oh, Master Barsby," I would say. "A charming boy, but he needs to grow up."

So the weary weeks wore on until the buds began to appear. In the early summer, though, great upheaval came to our lives. The ladies of the household were called into the Countess of Malpas's chamber to hear an announcement. "There is to be a change in the king's household," she said. "Our mistress Queen Anne of Cleves is to be queen no more."

"What will happen to her?" I asked, aghast, visions of the fate of the former Queen Anne Boleyn flooding into my mind.

"And will there still be places for us at court?" was Katherine's question.

The countess told us that once the marriage was unravelled, the former queen would be called "the king's sister" and would retire from court.

"And you must give thought to your futures," the countess added in response to Katherine's question. "There won't be employment enough here for all of you." We turned to each other and murmured like doves in a cote upon hearing the bark of the fox.

The countess did not need to tell us that there would also be a major change in the constellation of the great men of the realm. Queen Anne's most powerful supporter, Lord Cromwell, was out of favour, and there was talk that he would even lose his head for having promoted this German match that had turned out so poorly.

Anne herself was not greatly dismayed by the news, and I suspected that she was looking forward to her freedom. This was a topic of conversation strictly for her private chamber. Her German staff and advisors were talking up the insult offered to their princess and their country. But everyone knew that this was a bargaining position to improve the money and status that the king would offer her to go quietly to her new country life.

She stayed firmly in her rooms on the ninth of July when we had a curious kind of party at court. All the great men of England had been summoned to put their names to a document. It stated that the marriage between the king and Queen Anne hadn't been consummated and that it was null and void.

"The queen has a great big void where her personality should be," Will Summers whispered, as we watched the courtiers trooping past us into the Great Chamber. "I'm not surprised that the king was disappointed." But he didn't look too upset, and the whole court was in a playful, almost festive, mood.

Later, in her chamber, the queen called me over to brush her hair. She, too, seemed happy, as relaxed as I had ever seen her, as if a burden had been lifted. If I were on the point of losing my crown, I would have been more regretful. But then, I understood that I enjoyed having some control over people and events, and that it made Anne nervous to command even me, her maid.

"Mistress Eliza," Anne said, as she laid down the brush. "You and I have always been friends." This was quite true, and we had often chatted together, officially to improve her English, but also for pleasure. "I know that your cousin Katherine finds me dull and prefers to be with my husband," she continued. At this, I kept my face carefully blank. "But you, you are a warm fire in a cold country."

I curtseyed, my heart genuinely full. But she

gestured me back to my feet and paused. I began to wonder what was coming next; clearly it would be important.

"When I leave court," she said, "I will have my own household. I shall live somewhere quiet in the country and have an easy life, with no great men or great events. I would like you to come with me. Of course, I will have no such high position as I have enjoyed here, but I think we could have a fine time together. We could sip wine, read books all day, and wander at liberty in the woods."

Again my heart glowed. She had judged me well in offering me three attractive prospects for the spending of our time. But I also knew at once, deep down, that I could not give up the court for such a life. My work here was not done, and my opportunities for saving Stoneton not yet exhausted. I remembered Will Summers's slow smile and his sketching out of what the future could hold for me.

"My *lady*," I said, my very words drawing attention to her reduced status. Until this day I had always called her "Your Majesty." "I fear that I would miss the court and the king too much to leave."

"I guessed as much, *mein Liebling!*" was Anne's generous reply. "Don't worry about it. I just hope and pray that this court and this king will be able to make you happy."

And so the German princess departed. Luckily, there was no suggestion from anyone at court that I should depart too.

Chapter 27

How to Have Fun

JULY 1540

My dear, I'm so pleased!"

The Countess of Malpas spoke more warmly than I could have imagined. It was as if I was speaking her language at last. "You are a good, hard worker," she went on, "once you have decided that a task is not beneath you. I'm sure you can learn how to have fun."

I had steeled myself to ask the countess for her advice. Freed from attending upon the silent German queen, my time had once again become my own, and I decided to take the plunge and use it differently. No longer would I spend my leisure with books or by myself. Following Master Summers's suggestion, I would set out to enjoy myself and see what would happen.

"Now then," she said, sitting me down at her table and spreading a pack of cards before us. "You should probably learn Pope Paul — that's the most fashionable game. Lord! To think that you've been at court a whole year and haven't learned how to play it! I sometimes wish that I could stay away from the table myself, but it *is* such fun. I can lend you this for placing bets, but mind you pay me back by Michaelmas. Your cousin already owes me money." The countess pushed a stack of golden coins towards me.

I also persuaded her to give me a new slot on the rota, so that I could come on duty an hour later in the morning and stay up later at night. Fortunately, little Anne Sweet had come to join us from Trumpton Hall, so she could take the early shift in the Great Chamber. I saved my energy for the evenings, when wine and gambling were in full flow.

And so, that summer, I made sure that I was the maid of honour who always had the best time. I laughed more loudly than anyone else, drank more wine, lost more money at cards to be sure, and wore fewer and tighter clothes. I had come to understand that my long skinny broomstick body was not necessarily worse than Katherine's curves. Some people even preferred it. I knew that the king's gentlemen could see the change in me, and I accepted with pleasure their admiration and compliments. There were no compliments to be had, though, from Henny, and I told her less and less about my doings.

Meanwhile, Katherine kept her distance, rarely laughing at my jokes or admiring the dresses I bought with my card-table winnings. She did not often seem to be in the public rooms, nor was she much in the maids of honour's waiting room during our time off.

Once I glimpsed her through the window, walking in the gardens with Ned Barsby. The sight of his tall figure ambling along, hands behind his back, his fair head bent attentively towards Katherine, made me feel sick inside. She was performing her usual nauseating turtledove act, cooing senselessly as she did with all the men. In the past, Ned had told me he despised it, but now I saw him throw back his head to laugh at something she'd said. That evening, during my dressing, I snapped at Henny for her clumsiness.

But mainly I dealt with Katherine by making the most of her absence and asserting myself. At last, at long last, I felt myself to be the maid of honour most in demand. At archery I insisted that I should be the one to give the signal to the king to release an arrow, and he good-naturedly obeyed my commands. When we went out on the river, I yelled at the watermen to go faster. And at night I danced the silly trembling "Dance of the Gentle Fawn" in the Great Chamber and made everyone laugh.

And every day I felt the king's eyes rest upon me for perhaps a little longer.

My greatest success came in the bowling alley. I was wearing a new green dress, loose enough just to slip off the curve of my shoulders, but tightly laced around my waist. Instead of being cut low at the front, as Katherine's dresses were, it was cut low at the back, and revealed what the Countess of Malpas called the "elegant column" of my spine. Once again Katherine was missing. "Oh, I think she must be resting," said the countess when I asked. "She was on duty very late last night." This left me uneasy. To which intimate court circles had Katherine gained admittance, while I was left excluded? Was she expecting a betrothal, and if so to whom?

But I didn't really care, as long as I was making progress with the king.

And today Katherine's absence could give me the chance to shine. To the horror of the crusty old dukes and duchesses, when the wild mood took him, the king was more than glad to drink ale with his butler and play games with even his lowest servants. The court had assembled at the alley after taking wine, and the king was bawling out that he was bored of all his gentlemen. "Today," he yelled, "I deserve a frolic."

The Countess of Malpas and I exchanged glances. This could be interesting. The king's frolics alternated between the riotous and the dangerous. But then His Majesty's next words filled me with dismay. "I'll frolic with Master Ned Barsby," the king boomed out. "Come out, sir! Come down here and let me thrash you!"

The courtiers were crowded into the end of the long narrow alley, and some of us had even squeezed ourselves along its sides to the grave danger of our toes once the balls were in motion. My own position was against the wall, right up at the far end near the pins. From here I had a fine view of the whole crowd, and I could see clearly as Ned pushed his way forward. People were reaching up to tousle his hair and pat him on the back or even, in the case of Master Summers, to put him in a playful headlock. There were chuckles and whoops. I realised, a little ruefully, just how popular Ned was at court. And I had sternly been telling myself for weeks now that he was a forgettable nobody.

First the king rolled, and then Ned rolled, then it was the king's turn again. The hollering and cheering grew louder as the game became tense. I could tell that Ned was trying his best to offer a reasonable match but not to win: everyone knew that to beat the king was dangerous. Ned fooled around as he bowled a second time, flailing his arms wildly, pretending to lose his balance, but nevertheless performing deceptively well. Yet not well enough to win outright. The two balls ended up almost at the same spot at my feet near the pins. But which was nearer?

"Mistress Eliza will tell us who has won!" the king called out. I had been standing quietly, observing rather than entering into the boisterous mood of the crowd. I decided that the safest course was to maintain my pose as an ice maiden. I determined to spin the matter out, pretending to be uncertain which ball was closer to the pins, but taking it deadly seriously.

"I need to measure you both," I said, removing the necklace I wore and using it to calculate the distance like a yardstick. I must admit that I enjoyed the fact that everyone was watching and waiting for my verdict; for a moment the whole court was silent and panting. It felt like I held them all in the very palm of my hand.

"It's close," I said. "Master Barsby is better at rolling a ball than he is at brushing his hair."

At this the court erupted into laughter, and Ned himself clapped his hands over his head. I felt my own lips twitching, but I kept up my cool demeanour. The king had his arm now around Ned's neck, now slapping him on the back. For a second, elated with the game, the king looked young again and hearty and handsome as the Countess of Malpas told us he had once been when he was fresh to the throne. Something of Ned's rosy good spirits had rubbed off upon him.

"But it's close indeed!" I continued, the court falling silent for my words. Calls of "Shh!" and "Quiet!" rang out through the alley as I made some further spurious measurements with my necklace, pretending to consider the matter carefully. Eventually, I sank down on to one knee and dipped my head to the king. I paused theatrically, then raised my chin.

"Your Majesty is the victor!" I pronounced. The crowd, predictably, exploded with delight.

"I must keep the lucky necklace," the king said, stumping up to me and holding out his hand. "I shall give you another to replace it, as a gift." Holding my eyes, he lifted my necklace to his lips and popped it round his neck inside his shirt. When the king finally broke his gaze, I noticed that Ned's face was such a picture of disapproval that he might almost have been Aunt Margaret. A nasty prickling feeling started up in my stomach, and I had to turn away.

After that, we all began to crowd out of the bowling gallery and on towards the tennis court for further games and gambling. As I lifted my foot to step over the threshold, though, I glanced back and noticed that Ned had remained behind.

He was standing there quietly at the head of the bowling alley, eyes to the floor, and rubbing the back of his neck where the king's arm had been.

But then he lifted his head and saw me. I raised my eyebrows, inviting him to speak.

He's going to apologise for giving me that miserable look, I told myself. *He knows that it's my job to please the king. He must know I've done nothing wrong.*

In fact, it struck me that he'd been rather mean in failing to acknowledge my role in making the game a success for the court. The thought made me stand up taller. I wanted him to recognise my skills as a courtier. And what else did he expect me to do in a situation like that?

As I waited, I raised my hand and felt my exposed collarbone. My necklace had gone, but the memory of the king's eyes burning into the hollow at the base of my throat still persisted. It gave me a glow of confidence.

I stood there for a moment longer, but Ned said nothing at all.

Chagrined, I grabbed Will Summers's elbow, and we flounced away together into the sunshine.

I felt that matters were going well for me as the month of July played itself out. I was delighted to receive a package sent over from the royal lodgings that contained a silver locket with the letter "H" carved upon it. I wore it every day, and the holiday mood at court continued. With Queen Anne's uncomprehending and darkly dressed figure removed from the top table, our evening dances and japes became more and more wild and risqué. The only unmentionable subject was the fate of Lord Cromwell. He had forfeited his honours, and it was whispered that he now lay in the Tower of London awaiting his certain execution. For myself, I could hardly bear to think of such dark things during these bright days and largely succeeded in putting the matter from my mind.

As the weeks went by, I more and more often exchanged lingering glances with the king. I felt it was only a matter of time until he would give me the signal to come to him privately.

Chapter 28

To Marry Again

One night in late July, the nightingales were singing and the courtiers had trooped out into the park to listen — or, at least, to pretend to listen, while taking the chance in the dark to put their arms around the willing waists of the maids of honour.

But Katherine and I for once had both decided to remain in the palace. The king had declared himself tired and retreated to his secret rooms. Without him the nightingale expedition seemed to me to have little point. It would have been a waste of face powder.

So we ended up alone together in the waiting chamber. Perhaps it was because matters had been going well for me that I was content to sit peaceably with Katherine as the light faded. We worked over all the current court gossip, and I was struck anew by her penetration. "Malpas is soft as butter if she knows what's going on," Katherine said, "but she's hard as marble if she thinks you're keeping a secret." At this, she looked coy, and I sensed that she wanted me to ask what she meant. But I was too proud to play her game.

Even so, she did have an uncanny understanding of people's characters, and in spite of myself, I almost enjoyed the evening. At last, though, one or the other of us yawned, and silence fell.

"Feeling pleased with yourself?" she suddenly asked me in her offhand manner. "Are matters back on with a certain Master Barsby?"

"That's for me to know and for you to find out!" I trilled, continuing to twirl a curl of my hair round my finger while peering at my reflection in the windowpane. In reality I had succeeded in avoiding Ned altogether since the incident at the bowling alley.

H*a!* I said to myself, as I turned to inspect my profile. *You think you know everything, Katherine, but the king hasn't given you a necklace.*

The thought made me smile, and for once Katherine misread it.

"I'm glad for you," she continued with unexpected sincerity. "Although he's only a page, he's a kind man." I quickly turned towards her in order to remonstrate, for I did not want rumours of a relationship circulating the court. It might deter the king.

But she gave me no chance to speak. "And I, too, have some good news," she went gaily on. "Let me tell you now, for the whole court will be told tomorrow, and all my relatives should have the information in advance."

"Indeed? What's the news?" I said carelessly, interested, but in no manner alarmed.

"The king is to marry again, very soon indeed!" she said triumphantly.

"No!" I said. She certainly had my full attention now, and my brain whirred as I slipped off the window seat and stepped towards the chair where she lolled. "Really? Are you sure? Who's the bride? Katherine, this is a joke. I don't believe you. How do you know?"

She got up from her chair and placed her hands on her hips in that characteristic aggressive stance, and I saw that dangerous sleepy smile cross her face. "I have very good reason to know exactly who the lady is, and she's someone you yourself know very well."

I stood there shrugging and beginning to grow a little impatient with her game. "Well, don't tell me then," I said, as I perceived that she wanted me to beg her, and I had no intention of doing so.

Then she said the words that caused my stomach to lurch into astonished confusion.

"Little Eliza, little cousin Carrots." She laughed. "The king has asked *me* to marry him!" she said. "I am going to be the next queen!"

Chapter 29

Made to Look a Fool

JULY 1540

On the twenty-eighth day of July, at the Palace of Oatlands, my cousin Katherine married the king.

Of course she was as meek as milk in public, but once we were out of the public gaze, in the queen's own apartments overlooking the park, her triumphant crowing and queenly airs made me almost ill with jealousy. I was sickened too by my own sense that I'd been made to look a fool. Having set out to entrap the king, I'd been beaten at my own game. And of course it was Katherine who had beaten me. Whatever she wanted, she would take. She would always win.

I tried to act as if I hadn't a care in the world during our week at Oatlands, the small and private pleasure palace surrounded by parks and gardens and a green glassy moat.

I danced and swayed with the ladies, flirted with the men, even brought myself to simper at the king himself. But he now had eyes for no one but Katherine, and her hand was never out of his. No one knew how long their relationship had been more than was strictly proper between sovereign and subject, and Katherine wasn't saying. The king was utterly besotted and constantly called her his "rose without a thorn."

It was very bitter for me to experience my cousin's triumph. All over the palace, courtiers were to be heard sharing their astonishment that such a young woman, indeed a girl only two years older than me, could have brought off such a coup.

It was even harder to swallow the situation alone. There was simply no one to whom I could talk about it. Ned had shown his disdain for the dilemmas of a maid of honour, and in any case I had not spoken to him for weeks. The Countess of Malpas was wreathed in delighted smiles and claimed that she had known all along. And I'm pretty sure that behind their animated social masks, the rest of the unmarried maids—barring sweet Anne Sweet—were feeling as sick inside as I was myself.

I now remembered the advice my father had given me, which had been backed up by Will Summers. I reviewed my own plan of action and realised that although I had made the right moves, I had left it too long and begun too late. And Katherine had gone even further than becoming the king's mistress. Somehow, using the fabled charms of her body and mind, she'd persuaded him to make her his queen. It seemed astonishing.

But then I remembered Queen Anne Boleyn, who'd pulled a similar trick. Anything could happen at court. I'd had my own opportunity, I'd lacked Katherine's boldness, and I'd squandered it.

After the court's late nights, I woke groggy and sleepy, unwilling to face a new day. Dear Henny would bring me a cup of hot milk, just like the old days. The difference was that she would now place it silently by my bed, rather than scold me into drinking it. One morning I opened my eyes to find her sitting right by my bed, one hand on the coverlet. She must have been watching me sleep. The sight of her solid, kindly form made my throat tighten and my eyes prick. But neither of us spoke.

With an air of great condescension, Katherine had asked me, as her cousin, to remain in her household as a maid of honour. Thinking grimly of my father, the poverty of our home, and the unfinished business of finding a husband for myself, I reluctantly agreed. In the queen's household, my chances of finding a rich husband could only be increased. Now that the king was married, I must revert back to my original plan.

There had been a great influx of our relations to Oatlands Palace for the wedding. There was the old duchess, Katherine's grandmother, our cousins from Trumpton, and my own father and aunt. It seemed that everyone in England related to the Howards had turned up to see what pickings could be found now that our girl wore the crown.

Anne Sweet was to be a maid of honour in the new household of the queen, just like myself, and indeed I was glad of her company. But the sight of another familiar face from Trumpton Hall astonished and horrified me.

A few days after the wedding, I was turning the pages of a music book in Katherine's private chamber late in the afternoon, glad for once to be by myself and reluctant to go down to the chapel for prayers as I knew I should. It was a strain pretending all the time that everything was wonderful, and I just wanted nothing more than to lie down and sleep for a week.

I was disturbed by a masculine cough, and I looked up, startled, for no men were supposed to stray into the queen's apartments. At Oatlands, the royal rooms were secluded in a new wing with a wonderful view of the private park, and they were not overlooked by any other suite. I wondered that the guards had let anyone in. For a moment, a fearful thought of French spies or assassins flitted across my mind.

"Sir!" I called out. "Step forward so that I may see who you are! I must see you to know whether you may be here or not."

To my surprise, there was something familiar about the figure who stepped out from behind the loop of tapestry slung across the door. Yes, I recognised that tuft of auburn hair and those strong and muscular calves. I recognised the peacock breeches and the musician's hands. It was Master Manham, carrying a stack of books and an inkwell, and trying and failing to bow to me politely with these impediments before him.

"I believe that the queen's new secretary may have access to her private rooms," he said with a smile. "It's delightful to see you again, Mistress Eliza! I am so glad that you are not yet a married countess or duchess, or whatever, and that we can serve the queen together."

I swallowed hard, unsure what to say. I was disgusted to see him again, for his handsome face brought back nothing but memories of shame. His dig at my unmarried status also gave me a sharp little pain, as if he had stepped on my toe.

But I was deeply troubled by what this development revealed about Katherine's own discretion. I was furious with her for bringing Master Manham to court, for she had placed me in an intolerable position. If the king were ever to discover that her former lover was here at the palace, what would he do? What would he do to those of us who had knowledge of his wife's youthful relationships? And did Katherine mean to pick things up where she'd left off?

As my face froze for a moment or two, I was afraid that he could see the whole sequence of my thoughts flitting across my face. "It's been a long time since we met at the Duchess of Northumberland's," he said loudly, as if to an audience.

But then he crossed the room to stand over me, the corners of the books in his arms almost poking my chest. The only word for his expression was menace. "What happened at Trumpton stays there," he said softly.

I knew that I must appear as frosty as a frozen lake. "I have not the slightest idea what you're talking about, Master Manham," I said, lowering my lashes. "Let me help you with those books."

Shortly afterwards, I used the excuse of Mass to retreat to the gloom of the chapel and the blessed requirement of silence.

By some unlucky chance, though, I found Ned beside me in the pew as the voices of the choir lit up the summer evening.

"Eliza!" he whispered. "Are you all right?"

It was the first time in weeks that he had spoken to me, and as I turned it was a shock to see his face, so familiar, so close to mine. A pleasant smell, like green grass, came off him, and I noticed that he'd had his hair cut. But as well as realising that I missed Ned, it was doubly painful that he could tell I was upset. I couldn't bear to have anyone commiserate with me.

"Of course I am!" I hissed back like an angry cat, although there was a burning feeling in my throat. To clear my eyes, I fixed them firmly upon one of the golden cherubs decorating the rafters, as if I were contemplating the Almighty.

"My apologies for asking," he said with cold formality, and turned his face away.

Out of the corner of my eye, I noticed that Anne Sweet was on his other side. And I could not help noticing too that Ned handed her a prayer book and extended his arm to help her back to her feet after we had knelt. Obviously little Anne, the newcomer, had taken my place as Ned's friend.

Despite my best efforts, a scalding hot teardrop insinuated itself between the cherub and my vision. "Don't let it run down my cheek," I silently begged the Almighty. "I can't cry here. He mustn't see me crying."

I suddenly remembered how warm and lovely it had felt in the old days when Ned had enfolded me in his arms at the merest hint that I was unhappy. The feeling struck me hard, like a blow between the shoulders. I staggered and swayed as we stood.

"Dear Lord," I prayed when the time came to kneel. "Being in prison couldn't be worse than this. Please, please, release me from my life."

Part Four

To the Tower

Chapter 30

Jaded

SUMMER 1541
ELIZABETH IS SEVENTEEN . . .

A year later, I had forgotten all the pleasure I had taken in the position of maid of honour as I had held it under Queen Anne. There was no more gossiping behind the scenes as there had been with her, or kind whispered words to smooth the passing of hours of dutiful service in public. With Queen Katherine, it was "fetch this" and "clean that" in private, while before the court it was business as usual: smiling, curtseying, offering refreshments, dancing, and gambling. I had grown a sort of prickly shell to protect myself from the world. I felt safer within it, but I was lonely. I realised that my cold and offhand manner, my pretence that I cared about nothing, repelled my enemies, but also my friends.

I had never thought that I might become jaded with the magnificent palaces of Hampton Court and Greenwich, places that had at first seemed like a paradise. But I was tired of the endless luxury of our life and our stifling lack of air and freedom. I was tired of watching my cousin sitting with such majesty in the Great Hall on feast days and sitting without inhibition on the king's knee, like a jolly barmaid, when the senior courtiers had retired to the Great Chamber.

"She's been a very clever girl after all," said Will Summers softly while we watched her tickling the king underneath his greying whiskered chin.

Master Summers had been one of the few people at court whom Katherine had failed to conquer, and I had set much store by his never having been able to see the point of her. So his admiration for her strategy seemed doubly galling to me now.

At least it was time for a change of scene. We were to set off on one of the great summer progresses around his country that the king liked to undertake to show himself to his subjects. We would all go, sleeping in noblemen's castles, in their stables, or in hastily erected tents in the fields outside, just as our status decreed.

For the other maids of honour and me, the work and preparation of Katherine's — no, Queen Katherine's — wardrobe was enormous. We seemed to be packing for days, trunking up tapestries, cushions, and bedding as well as her gowns. I could not imagine how long our train of horses and wagons would be once we were finally on the road.

I was glad that the ultimate destination of our progress was to be York in the north, and that we would therefore travel through my home county of Derbyshire. We were to hop from house to great house, giving all the courtiers the chance to show their hospitality to the king. It was considered a great honour to have him to stay, even though it would be cripplingly expensive for each host to provide the whole court with food and lodging and entertainment. Some noblemen had even been known to bankrupt themselves building fine new wings to their houses, simply in the hope of having the king come to visit.

It was Katherine herself who told me what the itinerary was to be, while she was wallowing in her monthly bath. Anne Sweet and I were red-faced and exhausted, having spent about an hour bringing in the jugs of hot water to fill the tub, scenting the bathwater with herbs, and digging out Katherine's special olive oil soap, which we had accidentally packed away too soon. I shuddered to think how much each ball had cost.

"Oh, Eliza," she trilled as she splashed about in the water. "I know something you don't know!" I was on my knees getting out and unfolding her linen towels, and hardly in the mood for her guessing games. "Do hand me the other soap, will you, the one with the violet scent," she said, hauling herself half out of the water and extending a plump arm. As always, Katherine had no modesty and refused to wear a linen shift in the bath as Queen Anne of Cleves had always done. I averted my eyes and handed the new soap to her as she let the old one dissolve and be wasted in the water.

"It's about the progress," Katherine continued, sinking back with a sigh of pleasure and sloshing water over the floor. "Last time the king was in Derbyshire, with that simpleton Queen Jane, he stayed with the Earl of Westmorland." She paused to lather an armpit. I lifted my head from the linen and tensed myself for what might come next. Of course I knew all too well that he had stayed at Westmorland, for I had been there myself on the same occasion, getting into trouble.

Fortunately, though, Katherine didn't seem to know about that. "I told Hen that it would be most comfortable to stay there at Westmorland again," she said. "But he said that sometimes, as king and queen, we have to suffer for our duty. We have to stay in all sorts of horrible places, even if it means sleeping in a pigsty, so that these local aristocrats won't get jealous of each other. So we can't stay at Westmorland two progresses in a row."

Despite my annoyance at her "we" and "us" and her "Hen" for the king, I began to hope what she might be going to say. Abandoning the towels, I rose to my feet.

Katherine laughed out loud at my eagerness. "Yes!" she said. "We're going to that squalid little sheep farm where you grew up, Eliza."

"Oh, Eliza! Stoneton! We're going to see your home!" said little Anne Sweet, squeezing my arm in pleasure.

But Katherine, of course, could not tolerate Anne's kindness or my pleasure, and chose that moment to surge up out of the water.

"Come on, maids, where's my towel?" she demanded, standing there stock-still and naked, with soapy water spilling off her fleshy flanks.

Anne and I had to rootle on the floor for the towels and gently and respectfully pat her dry. I did it dutifully, but it made my own flesh creep.

Chapter 31

An Enemy in Real Life

SUMMER 1541

It was a bright, gusty morning, and my little white nag was climbing valiantly up the steep hill. I had forgotten how stony and how bracing our own county of Derbyshire was in its land and in its air. My stomach had been churning ever since Stoneton's towers had appeared on the skyline. This visit should have been the highlight of the whole month of travelling, changing scenery, and extravagant festivities. I was coming home!

But then again, I was coming home empty-handed. I'd been sent out into the world to find a husband, and I'd failed. My heart kept rising then sinking again like the dips in the road.

Anne was riding alongside me, and she laughed out loud at my obvious pleasure as I pointed out various landmarks to her. I felt that I should reintroduce a note of reality.

"I'm a bit worried, Anne," I said. "You see how steep these meadows are. And the sheep are pretty thin, aren't they? Everyone's going to guess that our estate isn't really up to paying for royal guests. I know my father will spend money we haven't got to maintain the honour of the Camperdownes. He might even sell *me* to pay for the king to have a good time."

"Ah, but, Eliza," she replied, holding on tight as her own horse skidded a little on the gritty track, "surely all your family's friends will have helped him out with extra food and loans of furniture? The visit's an honour to the whole neighbourhood."

If it had been anyone other than Anne, who was never annoyed, I would have said that there was a note of frustration in her voice. "Just for once,

Eliza," she said, "why don't you try to relax and enjoy yourself?"

Of course she was right. But my lurching stomach wouldn't let me. "Oh, Lord!" I sighed. "And he's going to ask me whether I'm likely to be married soon. Do you think he'll wait until I'm even off my horse?" I could not get rid of my nerves.

"Oh, but all fathers are the same," said Anne. "At least if their daughters are maids of honour. I hardly dare open letters from mine!"

The king, the queen, and the maids of honour were the last to arrive at each destination on our progress, all the preparations having been made in advance of us. The old castle ahead of us wore a holiday air. There were colourful pennants fluttering from every pinnacle, and a great scarlet swag of silk hung down over the gateway. All along the roadside were our farmers and tenants, and sometimes I even heard my own name called out from well-wishers among the crowd. Completely abandoning the idea that I was a sophisticated court lady, and should therefore never reveal my teeth, I grinned like a loon.

That night I left my place between my father and Aunt Margaret at the table, and slipped out of the supper in the noisy Great Hall to wander along the battlements. I wanted a moment alone to remember the little girl I'd been when I lived here before and to wonder at the changes that had taken place to her since.

Of course I was hardly alone; the place was bristling with guests and guards. But I needed a second or two to examine the feelings, happy and sad, which had come rushing over me in successive waves as I talked to my father, my aunt, old Mr. Nutkin, and young Mr. Steward. All of them were pleased and proud that our cousin was now queen and that I was with her in the royal party. And yet I felt that they were all too kind to mention their disappointment that I myself was not yet married.

Without my paying too much attention to where I was going, I found my feet taking me up the circular staircase to the top of the highest tower. I realised a little late that others, of course, would want to see the stars and breathe the night air as well, and the little platform was already occupied.

As he turned towards me, I was stunned to see that the dark shape against the sky was Ned Barsby.

I nearly turned and went straight back down, but it was too late. He was speaking.

"So this is where you grew up!" he said, gesturing down to the jumble of slate roofs below, illuminated by torches and expensive wax candles within, and by the last glimmers of a summer dusk without. He had spoken easily, as if without thought. In a moment the long silence between us was broken, and of course he had done it.

He puts people at ease, I thought. *It's his gift.*

I stepped across to stand next to him, suddenly feeling more like myself than I had for ages.

"Yes," I said, looking down. "It seems such a hotchpotch of a place now that I've seen Hampton Court. But still I find that I love it." Whether I felt comfortable to be back at home or just comfortable to be with Ned, he seemed to sense that tonight I wasn't going to bark or bite.

"Look over there!" he said, pointing out to the distant hills, and then steadying me against the battlements as I leaned forward.

"What am I looking at?" I asked, although I wasn't all that bothered. The warmth of his body as he'd stepped close to me was strangely attractive, and he put his arms around me from behind.

"Well, maybe it's nothing," he said, his chin brushing the top of my hair. "I thought I saw a falling star."

We stood there for a while in companionable silence, and there seemed to be a distant beating of a drum. Gradually, I realised that it was my heart. *How foolish*, I thought, *it's only Ned*. Only a page. Only an old friend. But still he was standing very near to me.

Now he was mumbling something into my hair, touching it with his lips. I could feel his breath warm on my neck.

"What's that?" I said.

"I miss you, you know," he said, more distinctly. "I hate not seeing you like I used to. I've been looking forward to coming here to Stoneton just to learn more about where you come from."

Before I could respond, there was the scuff of a foot on the stone stairs. For a moment—which felt like it was ten years long — we stood frozen at the battlements, not knowing what to do.

When we finally sprang apart, it was jaggedly awkward.

Francis Manham was there in the dark doorway. He stepped out to join us, hands on hips, his head to one side. "Ah, Mistress Elizabeth," he said, with a cool glance at Ned. "They told me you'd been seen climbing up here. I didn't realise you had an assignation."

"Well, it wasn't . . ." I said foolishly, trailing off into silence as I realised that it would have been wiser not to try to defend myself.

Two friends might stand together watching a falling star. But friends did not stand as close as we had done, nor for so long. My blood was still singing. Ned's embrace had sent it flooding into my cheeks. They must have glowed like flames in the dark.

"Anyway, I'll say nothing," he said. "A moment alone, Mistress Eliza, if you will. I need some information."

There was a long pause during which Master Manham stared at Ned. I glanced between the two, noticing that Ned was not only half a hand-span taller, but sparer and leaner as well. Master Manham was so well built that he was verging on the pudgy.

"It's all right, Ned," I said reluctantly. Our moment was over; it was useless to try to recapture the spell. And surely I would be safe. What harm could come to me in my own home?

Ned's eyes searched my face anxiously. I nodded. He gave a low and icy bow to Master Manham and went off down the stairs, whistling insouciantly.

"Whippersnapper!" said Master Manham as the sound faded. "Who does he think he is? An insolent bastard page boy like him!"

I wanted to say I preferred a bastard like Ned to a man like him, but I made no reply. My fists clenched themselves into balls, my nails digging deep into my palms. My blood still blazed, and I did not trust myself to speak with a steady voice.

"Now," he said, "to business. The queen tells me that you know something about a secret passage to her chamber. She wants me to deliver some important papers to her later tonight, without disturbing the king."

A secret passage? The sally port! He was right, it did exist. But how on earth did they know?

I thought hard.

Then, for the umpteenth time, I cursed my propensity for showing off. I now remembered telling all the girls at Trumpton Hall my stories about growing up at Stoneton and about our sally port too. Katherine would naturally have remembered, just as she stored away in that brain of hers any information that could be of use. Scheming cow.

I needed to buy myself some time to think. "I believe you should ask my father," I said, trying to edge my way towards the entrance to the stairs. I was bound to do what my mistress, the queen, demanded of me. But I was not at all convinced that the king would want me to help a man get into his wife's room at night.

"No, not so fast, Mistress Elizabeth," he said, laying a hand upon my forearm. "You shall show me yourself."

Gradually, with increasing force, he backed me up against the stone of the battlement. Its corner was pressed painfully into the small of my back. I could see the tiny red-clad figure of a guard crossing the courtyard many head-spinning storeys below.

Should I shout for help? But that would cause a scandal. What had I been thinking, allowing myself to be trapped up here at the top of a turret, late at night, with such a man?

Anger and shame finally gave me the strength to tug myself free.

"I shall show you at once."

My whole body was shaking, but I managed to clip out the words. As we descended from the turret, my legs quivering like jelly, I remembered how I had once used to duel with imaginary knights up here for whole afternoons of play.

But now I had an enemy in real life, and he was right behind me on the stairs.

Chapter 32

A *Baby in Her Belly*

SUMMER 1541

That horrible night at Stoneton was only the beginning of an uneasy period for me. As the weeks of the royal progress rolled on, I gradually became certain that Katherine and Francis Manham were meeting up nearly every night. I also guessed that the other maids of honour must know of it, or at least suspect it. How could it be otherwise in the tight, incestuous world of the court?

In the houses where we stayed, there seemed always to be a sally port, as at Stoneton, or a secret passage or a back door to the close-stool room just waiting to be discovered and used by the lovers.

Katherine's boldness seemed breathtaking to me, but there was a certain logic to it. What she was doing was so wildly wrong, so patently mad, that it almost defied belief. Who would even countenance the possibility that the queen would dare to deceive the king? To cheat upon His Majesty would be a certain path to treason and death. So of course none of us maids of honour could even bring ourselves to mention it, let alone discuss it. The risks of being overheard were just too high. It was safer to pretend it wasn't happening.

There was something else of which we never spoke. Katherine had now been married a year, and each month we maids had to wash her shifts and her underlinens as they became spotted with blood from her menses. Of course we all appreciated the significance of this, and somehow the news got round the court too. On the day that her menses came, Katherine would snap and bite like a spoiled lapdog, and we all learned the hard way to submit at once to whatever humiliation or service she required.

Only one thing stopped me from confronting Katherine when she was in one of these moods and doing my best to gouge out her eyes with my fingernails. During our stay with the abbot of Lyddinghouse, I was on duty as the maid of honour selected to sleep on a camp bed outside the queen's bedchamber door. I did not mind this duty at all, for it was a cramped and miserable business sharing a bed with two or even three bedfellows in the limited accommodation of these borrowed houses. I like a bit of space and quiet in which to think my thoughts and sometimes read my book in my little pool of candlelight.

In the abbot's house, my camp bed had been made up in a stone cloister that reminded me of my home. Although the space was cold and echoing, I had furs and blankets to keep me warm, and I could hear the comforting sound of the guards laughing together some way off around the turn of the passage.

As I dozed off that night, though, the peace was broken by a ragged sigh from inside the queen's room. Then another. I sat up, stiff as a board, transfixed with horror.

My first thought was that Katherine must be ill, and I nearly got out of bed to go to her.

Then, as I strained my ears in the silence, I realised that she was weeping. All at once I remembered that this afternoon she had called for linen cloths. Putting two and two together, I realised that she wished she had a baby in her belly, and that she was rightly worried that the rest of the court was wondering why she did not. I thought about going in and attempting to comfort her. But I was fairly certain that Katherine's pride would mean that she'd rather I didn't.

My glimmerings of pity for Katherine, though, were erased the very next day. Anne and I went along to her chamber in the early evening to do our usual work. Finding the room deserted, I busied myself by picking up the nightgown Katherine had left lying on the floor and putting the pins straight in her pincushion, while Anne was pulling the hairs from her brush.

"So how was it?" Anne asked.

"How was what?" I replied with a gruffness I did not really feel.

I knew Anne had seen me in the abbot's herb garden that afternoon, walking and talking with

Ned. I had been picking petals for a potpourri when he came out to join me. The sun had tempted all of us to shed some of our usual courtly finery, and his doublet was slung over his shoulder. Ned's shirt was open and a few hairs were visible on his chest. I had never seen so much of his skin before, and although there was nothing particularly improper about the way he was dressed, it seemed as shocking to my senses as nakedness. My eyes returned again and again to his chest as we talked of this and that, wandering between the flower beds. It was wonderful to be friends again. Despite our long estrangement of months past, I found myself interrupting what he said and teasing him as easily as if he were Henny. Nobody made me feel as light and airy inside as he did.

It was with a guilty start that I'd noticed Anne smiling at us from across the garden, and I'd thought it strange that she did not come to join us.

"Eliza," she now said seriously, "you should not lead him on, you know. He cares for you."

I furrowed my brow. Anne, little Anne, was daring to criticise me? On such a personal matter too?

"And how do you know all about it, sweetie?" I asked, carefully careless in my tone and bending over the dressing table so that she could only see my back.

"Ned's my friend," she said in her simple manner. It was guileless and unanswerable, yet I, too, would have described Ned as a "friend" to any bystander. What a range of emotions that word could cover. I felt a twinge of conscience. Yes, I'd been friendly towards Ned, but how would I feel if Aunt Margaret, for example, had seen us talking and flirting in the sunshine? Guilty and wrong was the answer. I knew that I shouldn't have been wasting my time on such a pointless pursuit.

And yet I felt that more than anything I would like to spend the evening ahead sharing a cup of wine with Ned in that garden as dusk fell. All I wanted was to be with him. I couldn't stop myself.

My thoughts were interrupted by a little sound from the close-stool room in the corner. Glancing over, I saw that its door stood closed, and I assumed at once that the necessary woman had come in through the outside service door to take away the chamber pot and to clean the room. Each day she needed to lay out fresh napkins and maybe place a vase of scented roses on the windowsill.

But the sound grew and turned into scuffling and then giggling. It was unavoidable that Anne and I should acknowledge it. We stood in the middle of the room staring at each other, frozen in doubt and dismay. Anne still had the queen's hairbrush held uselessly in her hand.

A few seconds later, Katherine herself burst through the close-stool room door back into the bedchamber, her face flushed. On seeing us, she checked herself and grabbed the brush from Anne, banging at her hair with it and humming a little tune. I did not dare to ask who had been in the close-stool room with her, and who it was who now banged the outer door closed so loudly that we could all hear.

"Your face is a picture!" she said to me, smiling gaily. I knew that my cheeks were crimson, and I turned away in silence. All the pity I had felt when I'd heard her crying in the night was replaced with embarrassment.

And worse than that, fear.

Chapter 33

The Good Life I Lead with My Wife

2 NOVEMBER 1541

My eyes travelled over the ceiling. Its golden fretwork and golden cherubs glowed against a blue-painted background of sky, its construction swooping down into great bulbous knobs in an amazing feat of carpentry. And amid it all, the golden words: *Dieu, et mon droit.* God, and my right. The king had both of them on his side.

I sighed. Even the chapel ceiling at Hampton Court was a reminder to me of my duty: to obey God, to obey the king, to submit. But sometimes it was so very hard.

With a well-drilled rustle, the congregation sank to its knees. Coming to my senses, I found myself stranded in a standing position. I knelt down as quietly and smoothly as I could manage as the prayers began. We were at a special service at which the king was to give thanks for his marriage and the merry life he was leading with the queen. The queen! Despite all the months that had passed, I still couldn't quite get used to the fact that my cousin was the queen.

And I wasn't the only one. As the ripe phrases of the bishop rolled over us, extolling the sanctity of marriage, I caught Will Summers casting half a glance in my direction. He was down in the body of the chapel with the gentlemen of the court and had turned up and back to watch us maids of honour in our gallery with the queen. I studiously failed to acknowledge him. Will was taking a risk by removing his attention from the priest for even an instant, and I felt annoyed with him for compromising me.

It was essential to all our sanity to believe in the king's marriage and his great love for Katherine. Now that we were back at Hampton Court, there were at least no more secret passages or hidden doors as there had been in the strange houses we'd visited on the progress to the north. Here the security arrangements were as tight as could be, and whatever Katherine had been up to with her nocturnal visitor would have to come to an end.

I felt reasonably well rested, for I could now sleep much more peacefully at night, secure in the knowledge that I wouldn't hear a man's heavy footstep in the passage when no man should have been there. I was glad that Katherine had stopped asking me to dress her hair or hand me her pink lip salve even though it was bedtime. And I was pleased that she was no longer quite so hard to wake up in the mornings. I glanced sideways at her now, praying, a picture of demure piety. I could only admire her sangfroid.

She had good reason for smugness. Quite unlike the days of Queen Anne of Cleves, the queen's apartments were still busy in the late evenings, for the king was a constant visitor. When we saw the two tall yeomen standing outside the queen's bedchamber door with their spears, it was a sign that he had come to visit his wife. I would quickly turn around with the basin of water or cup of wine or fresh candle, or whatever it was I was carrying, and retreat out of sight and sound until it was safe.

Sometimes I might unwillingly overhear a laugh as I padded silently away, or else the king's great whooping coughs. He wasn't in what one would call good health, but Katherine had certainly improved him, making him happier, a little less snappy, and certainly a little less porky. In the early mornings, they would ride hard together out in the park. "Look!" the king would say in his disarming manner, as he came into the Great Chamber after these expeditions. "My rose without a thorn has taken inches off my waist."

Now we could hear the boards creaking in the king's own gallery next door, as he stepped forward to the front rail of his own closet. We could not see the king, but he prayed out loud, so that everyone could hear him.

"I give most hearty thanks," he said, sounding like he meant it, "for the good life I lead and trust to lead with my wife."

Anne Sweet, predictably, thought this was rather sweet. "Fifth time lucky!" she whispered into my right ear. To my left, I sensed Katherine straightening herself up even further and arching her back with pride.

Really! I thought to myself, sickened to my stomach. *I can hardly bear all this. It's intolerable. I'd be better off as a laundress or a farmer's wife.*

The king's thanksgiving for his marriage may have been the very worst moment of a life that was dull, unpleasant, and hard to bear during the whole of that autumn at Hampton Court. But little did I know that it had been a perfect paradise of bliss compared with what was to follow.

The very next day, Katherine's supposed cleverness caught up with her, and all of our lives were placed in danger.

Chapter 34

Just the Queen's Cousin

NOVEMBER 1541

The first we knew of the disaster was the appearance of one of the Yeomen of the Guard, with the news that the queen would not need anyone to dress her that evening.

This was unprecedented. We were all gathered in the countess's chamber, waiting for the call to come on duty. Some of the girls were doing embroidery, Anne was strumming a lute, and I was tracing out a family tree for the countess herself. She was in a tetchy mood, which made me think that news had come from home of some achievement of her little son's that made her miss him more than usual.

The yeoman stood red-faced and bowing in our midst. The end of his tall halberd knocked against the table where I worked and joggled my inkwell.

"Nonsense!" said the countess sharply. "Of course the queen will need dressing. And what are *you* doing here?" She meant that the message should not have been sent by a yeoman, his status being too low. "I don't want your clumsy and vulgar weaponry in my chamber," she added with a lofty wave of the hand.

"Forgive me, my lady," the man said, bowing low and looking so uncomfortable that I almost felt sorry for him. Indeed, there was a giggle from somewhere in the room, which made him blush even more. "I am only doing what I was told. I was commanded by the Lord Chamberlain to say that the queen's cousin is required. No one else. Just the queen's cousin."

There was a long drawn-out pause while everyone took in the tidings. The girl who had giggled turned it into a cough. This sounded like trouble, even danger. And I had no wish to be singled out or drawn into it. For a long while, my brain stubbornly refused to believe that by "the queen's cousin" he meant me.

I had no choice, though, but to go. Shrugging my shoulders at the countess, Anne, and the rest, to show them that I knew no more than they did, I reluctantly led the way down the stairs and into the courtyard. My steps were slow and heavy, and I could sense the poorly concealed impatience of the guard, compelled by etiquette to follow on behind me. His weapons and trimmings clanked slightly as he walked, something that I only noticed because the palace seemed strangely silent.

In the queen's chambers, I found Katherine as bemused as I was. "Oh, it's you," she said, as if disappointed.

"Well, who were you expecting?" When we were entirely alone, she did not insist upon "Your Majesty," though she was pretty keen on the full works if anyone else, even a page, were present.

"This is the time the king always sends me a message to see how I am," she explained, as if it were obvious. Once again I marvelled at his attentiveness to her— he'd never sent a message to Queen Anne to ask about her health when they were parted in the afternoons by his need to do business and meet his councillors.

"Katherine, what's going on?" I asked her. "That yeoman said that you would not be dressing tonight. Are you not going to dine?"

"I don't know," she said with unusual solemnity. "Something seems odd this afternoon. The palace is very quiet, isn't it? Where can everyone be?"

We had no answers. As one, we turned away from each other to look out at the trees in the park. I sat down on the ledge of one window, Katherine on the other, and we remained there quietly for some time. One of the trees, the nearest to our window, seemed diseased and drooping, and I was surprised the royal gardeners had not felled it.

It felt like hours later, but it was hardly fully dark, when the same yeoman came back again, this time his face looking as if he were positively in pain. He had brought with him the archbishop. The sight of this stooped old dignitary in a private chamber rather than a public place seemed to signal sickness or death or something else very bad indeed.

But it appeared that I was not to stay and hear what he had to say. The clanking yeoman marched me out of the room, brooking no delay, and escorted me back to the Great Chamber.

There I found all the rest of the queen's household gathered together, not just the ladies but the gentlemen too. By now little Anne Sweet was openly weeping, and the countess, looking harassed, was doing her best to comfort her.

"What news from the queen?" she asked me over the top of Anne's head. I noticed the creases round her eyes, which were normally hidden by the vivacity of her face.

"Nothing! She doesn't know what's going on either." At my answer, half a dozen voices piped up with further questions.

"Shush! Shush at once, you lot." I had never heard the countess's voice sound so harsh.

She had spotted that over near the door to the king's private apartments, the Lord Chamberlain was trying to call us to order. There were so many of us present that he'd had to stand on one of the benches, looking more than a little ridiculous. But no one thought, even for one moment, of laughing. Our hum of talk had been loud and shrill with nerves, yet we fell silent as soon as he opened his mouth.

"The queen will no longer require your services," he said into the silence.

"But why?" asked the Countess of Malpas on behalf of us all.

"The king has discovered that the queen has committed a dreadful crime," he said haltingly, obviously choosing his words with great care. "She will not come abroad from her apartments for some time to come."

A great buzz of consternation broke out from among the courtiers.

"The king, however, will still command you!" shouted the Lord Chamberlain over the din. Again we settled down, anxious to hear what he had to say. His next words came unnaturally loud, as if he had still been expecting to have to fight to be heard.

"His Majesty was at Mass when he learned this terrible news, and he remains in the chapel, praying for his wife. You will henceforth take your orders from him, through me. And none of you will speak of or to the former queen. She is under house arrest."

We stood in stunned silence, without a single sound except for Anne's snuffling.

Then we all heard a noise that none of us will ever forget as long as we live. We heard a terrible, unearthly shriek and the patter of running feet in the gallery adjoining the chamber where we stood.

"Henry! Henry!" It was hard to believe it was Katherine, this voice of uncontrollable, wild despair.

Instantly, there was a bark from the leader of the guards, and we heard men springing into action. There was the horrible clash of steel.

"How did she escape?" someone called out in anger. Then there was a different man's voice saying, "Come, madam, come, madam."

They must have been taking her back to her chambers. The footsteps receded in that direction, as did the sound of Katherine's sobs.

Chapter 35

Of Course There'll Be a Trial

Later that night, Anne and I were in our night-gowns but far from being ready to sleep. We had obeyed the Lord Chamberlain's command not to speak of the queen throughout the dinner that nobody ate, but once we were in our own room, we did nothing but whisper about our suspicions and our fears. "My father will be furious," said Anne. "What if I get sent away from court before I've found a husband?"

Looking down at Anne's frightened, vulnerable face as she knelt by the bed, engaged in a mixture of praying and crying, I mentally cursed Katherine.

What was it that she had been caught doing? Was it the very worst? Would she bring us all down with her? I knew that Anne's parents were kind and gentle, and I hardly dared think what my own father's reaction might be.

We were disturbed by the gentlest of scratches on the door. We were so wound up that we leapt as if at a thunderclap. I ran forward to pull it open, softly. Our visitor clearly wanted to make a discreet entrance.

I shrank back at the sight of a tall figure, cloaked in black, a beaked plague mask over its face.

"Lord preserve us!"

I really thought that Death himself had come visiting.

But Death barged forward into the room, pulled off his mask, and gave the welcome sound of a laugh.

"Oh, the look on your face, Eliza!" It was Will Summers.

"Oh, Will," said Anne reproachfully. "Whatever are you doing here? You know we're not allowed to have men in our chambers, especially at a time like this. It's so dangerous! What if you got caught?"

"Oh, well, if you don't want to hear what's happened . . ." he said nonchalantly, turning as if to go.

"Will!" I grasped his arm. "Don't listen to that scaredy-cat. Of course we do!"

"Well . . ." he began slowly, and with just a hint of relish.

I felt something a little like hatred for him then, because I could tell that, despite the stress of it all, the drama of the situation appealed to him.

"Just as the Lord Chamberlain said, the king was at Mass this afternoon when the archbishop handed him a letter. He had to be given a letter: that's what the councillors agreed. No one was brave enough to tell the king to his face that there is evidence to suggest that he has an unfaithful wife."

"Unfaithful!" Anne clapped her hand across her mouth, and her eyes were open as wide as windows during spring cleaning. "Well, that's a big accusation, isn't it? We all knew she had close friends. I think it must just be a misunderstanding."

Will snorted. "'Misunderstanding' is one word for it," he said scornfully. "'Adultery' is another.

Only you, Anne, could give her the benefit of so much doubt."

"And what did the king do then?" Despite herself, Anne could not restrain her interest.

"I wasn't there, you understand," Will said. "But I've heard it from those who were. The king read the letter, shaking his head as if in disbelief, and tore it in two. Some people say he stamped on the pieces, but that sounds like a dramatic embellishment, don't you think? Then the king turned to the archbishop with a look of daggers. But they say something stony in the old bishop's face convinced the king that this wasn't a malicious prank."

"So who do you think has betrayed her?" I asked. "I'm sure we maids of honour have not."

"I'll tell you what I think," said Will, shrugging. "I think that just about everyone else at court has betrayed her. It started very slowly, and then took hold, and now it's an inferno. Like a fire burning a house down. I don't think she'll find many men at court willing to vouch for her character. Be careful what you two say at the trial. If you say you knew nothing at all, it won't ring true."

"Trial!" Anne looked ready to faint.

"Yes, of course there'll be a trial," he said, slipping his beaked mask over his face once more.

"What do you mean, a trial?"

"Why!" Will said. "For treason, of course. Adultery, unchastity, any of that stuff, it's treason."

Anne and I stared each other, aghast. I reached blindly for the support of the post of our bed, for my legs had given way.

We had been worried that our court careers were over. But that now seemed an almost trivial concern compared with the possibility we hadn't even considered: that we ourselves might be put on trial for abetting treason.

Chapter 36

I Will Do My Duty

Will was only half right about who had betrayed Katherine. Yes, the case against her had gathered steam, as was inevitable in the gossipy furnace of the court, but the fire had to have started somewhere. As the archbishop's investigation took shape, it turned out that it wasn't the events of the progress to York that had caused the trouble. Or at least the beginning of the trouble. The courtiers knew better than to speak of that. The root of the problem lay back in the past, back at Trumpton Hall.

For Katherine should have married the king as an unsullied virgin. She should have been an innocent girl who had never known the touch of a man. For her to pretend this, as she had done, at the very least by omission, was certainly treason.

It seems that little Em, the serving wench from Trumpton Hall, had been the first to blab that Queen Katherine was not all she seemed. Once Master Manham was in the frame as a suspected lover of Katherine's, he revealed all, and there were rumours that the use of the rack had loosened his tongue about the details of Katherine's loss of her virginity. Little Em herself had lost her left ear in the course of the investigation.

Court gossip kept us informed of all these events, and with each new revelation my spirits fell further. During these terrible days of the trial, my eighteenth birthday came and went unheralded by anyone, except for Anne Sweet, who left a gingerbread heart on my pillow.

Finally, the day came when I myself was called in before the archbishop in the Council Chamber. I had been preparing myself for this moment ever since Will's warning, but even so my legs trembled violently as I passed along the gallery. I gouged my palms with my nails, forcing myself to focus upon the small sharp pain. That, at least, seemed manageable.

Inside the chamber, the dark hangings on the walls made the already dim November day seem like night.

I stood, waiting, my eyes cast to the floor, my fingers clasped together before me. It must have looked like a pose of submission, but really it was to stop my hands from shaking. When *would* the questions begin? It felt like hours were passing. I still did not dare to lift my eyes to see who my inquisitors were.

"You are the former queen's cousin? Seat yourself."

Surprised, I raised my head and saw that the archbishop was gesturing to the velvet-covered chair at the bottom of a long table covered with a rich Turkey carpet. He himself sat hunched over the table's top end, and all along its length was spread an infinite number of papers, letters, documents, and books. The expressionless faces of about ten other courtiers and privy councillors, whose seats lined each side, swivelled in my direction.

Some held their pens in midair, waiting for my answer before continuing with their writing.

I felt the colour rising to my cheeks under their gaze.

"Yes."

The word came out much louder than I was expecting. While I had been waiting, I had told myself not to crack, not to cry, with such fierceness that I may have gone too far in the other direction.

. . . so very young . . . His Majesty . . .

A clerk was bending over the archbishop's shoulder, whispering and handing him yet another document. I could not hear much of what he said.

"You have been maid of honour to the queen since her marriage?"

The archbishop reminded me of a hungry hawk, an elderly, scrawny version of the hunting birds I had seen sitting on the king's own wrist.

"Indeed I have, sir, and I hope I have given good service."

There was a pause. Again it seemed endless. My heart was now beating so loud, it sounded like someone hammering impatiently at a door. The archbishop was pulling his beard and cogitating. No one else spoke.

"Well, Mistress Camperdowne, we don't need your testimony against your mistress. We have quite enough evidence already."

Relief flooded through me, and while I tried to remain impassive, I'm sure it flickered across my face. One or two of the privy councillors now lost interest in me and returned their attention to the stacks of documents before them on the table.

"In fact," said the archbishop, looking again at his papers, "it appears that you can even be quite useful to us. It seems that His Majesty himself values your service. You will accept new duties from the king."

"Of course," I said in a tiny voice. It scarcely crossed my mind to wonder what these new duties might be. I was so relieved.

Now that the danger seemed to be passing, all the bravado went out of me. I fell back against the chair, limp as my old doll, Sukey. I almost whispered the words.

"New duties. Of course I will do my duty."

Chapter 37

At the Abbey

WINTER 1541

It wasn't exactly what I would have chosen, but it was far better than I had feared. I was told that I was to help to look after our former queen, becoming her maid once again, until her fate was finally decided.

That very same day, I packed to leave Hampton Court. I was to accompany Katherine to the old abbey at Syon. This was the place to which she was to be sent for safety and to pray, in seclusion, for her redemption.

I wasn't sure what to think about my new task, which was really my old task but under vastly changed circumstances. As Henny helped me to pack my chest, there was a quiet tap at the door. It was Ned. Henny bustled out of the room at once, murmuring something about towels left behind by the laundresses.

"Eliza!" he said urgently, almost before she had gone through the door. He was frantically rubbing his hair upwards with his hands. "Why are you going? Have you been commanded to go? Shall I take you away somewhere instead?"

"Oh, Ned!" I said. "You have made yourself look like a cockerel. Here, let me comb you down again. No, you mustn't take me away or you'll lose your place at court. And you really mustn't worry."

I gradually got him to stop pacing and explained that I didn't mind going with Katherine. "I'm almost eager to get out of here," I said. "There are so many whispers. People keep talking it over again and again, and there's nothing new to say."

Pragmatically, my head told me that I must show a willingness to serve the king's purposes. At the same time, my heart told me that I had something of a duty to my cousin.

"But I still don't see why *you* should have to go," he said, pacing about. "She's a traitor! You shouldn't have to be dragged in!"

"But, Ned," I reminded him, "the queen shares my own blood." At that I turned away from him to fold a shawl. It was not quite loyalty that I felt towards Katherine, and indeed it was a little late in the day to be feeling it, but I did feel something.

"Well, I can't feel sorry for her," he said angrily. "She has put you in danger."

"I don't expect you to understand," I said coldly. "I can't just put aside my family loyalty. How would that look? You'd understand if you were the heir to an old family yourself."

Even as the words left my mouth, I regretted them.

Ned's face, which had been full of concern, turned into a picture of hurt.

Then, all too soon, Henny was back again. Without another word, Ned moved quietly to the door and slipped out. Cursing my old enemy — my pride — I viciously threw a pair of shoes into the trunk. When they missed and fell to the floor instead, I swore under my breath.

***

Katherine was truly a pitiable creature as we made our way, the following day, through the gardens at Hampton Court to the riverside, in order to take our boat to the abbey. Syon was one hour's glide downstream from the palace and likewise placed on the banks of the Thames. As we went, Katherine kept looking back over her shoulder at the palace. She was almost drinking in the sight of it, as if to draw it indelibly upon her mind.

The slanting winter sun unfortunately high-lighted the fact that her hair was greasy and straggly, her eyes red with weeping, and her clothes dirty. As Katherine's only remaining maid, I was struggling to cope, and that morning I had not been able to per-suade her to change her linen. She had spent the early hours crying and pushing me away. At one point I'd managed to creep close enough to stroke her hair, but she'd burst out with a horrible deranged laugh that made me snatch back my hand. How different she was now, I thought, no longer to be envied, no longer to be feared. The queen of Trumpton Hall, as she had been, was no longer the queen of anything at all.

As the boatmen pushed us off the Hampton Court jetty, I saw that Katherine's gaze was still fixed upon the windows of the king's apartments.

"A magic spell has been cast upon my husband," she said softly, almost reasonably. "That's all. It cannot last much longer now, and then he will want me in his bed once more. God forgive me for what I will do to the witch who cast it, when I find her!" Then the boatmen started to beat their oars, and the palace passed out of sight.

At Syon, the weeks dragged by with unbearable slowness. While we knew that the investigation was progressing, we did not know what course it was taking.

One December afternoon I walked out in the abbey's leafless orchard, huddled inside my cloak against an angry wind, but glad to be breathing in fresh air for a change.

Our chamber inside the abbey had grown somewhat fetid. Katherine had so far refused to leave it, anxious, she said, not to miss any messenger coming from the king. This meant that it had been hard for the servants to clean it. We had been treated with great courtesy and dignity by these abbey servants. Katherine took this as no more than what was due to a queen, but I myself felt some shame. I could imagine the elderly steward and the similarly ancient cook-maid saying to themselves in the kitchens and corridors that we were just a couple of jumped-up girls who had misbehaved.

As I pushed my way through the long wet grass under the trees, I was enjoying the feeling of life returning to my legs and entertaining myself by finding and counting the few shrivelled and spotted apples still clinging to the black branches. Then I noticed out of the corner of my eye a slight, dark female figure.

I guessed that perhaps it was one of the nuns expelled from this place by the Lord Cromwell, come back for some reason unknown. The sight of a stranger in the abbey orchard made me uneasy. The place was so ancient and so quiet that it even crossed my mind that perhaps it was the spirit of one of the nuns of old, walking abroad. But not in full daylight, surely?

The wind whipping my hair around my face and neck obscured my view of the woman approaching, but she was quickly coming towards me. She materialised into Anne Sweet, heavily wrapped in a black cloak, and her head muffled in a dark-coloured shawl.

"Anne!" I said. "What are you doing here? You will be in trouble!"

"It's all right, Eliza," she said, breathing a little heavily as she glanced around in all directions. "My escort is at the edge of the woods there. No one saw us arrive, and, in any case, the countess knows I am here. How are you, Eliza? You look tired. I'm sure I would look like a corpse if I was as pale as you are, but those violet stains under *your* eyes look rather romantic."

I was so pleased to see a friendly face, I could have cried. Anne, true to her nature, discerned that I was too proud to ask for a hug, so she hugged me anyway. "We are all worried about you!" she whispered into my ear. "It's so good to see you."

Eventually she pulled away, and we went to sit on a stone seat in the shelter of the orchard wall, clearing it as well as we could of its heaped, rotting leaves.

"What news of Katherine's trial?" was my next question.

Anne had little to tell me. "They're keeping it from all the former members of her household," she said. "They may yet call us back to give further testimony, you know."

At that I shivered.

"Do you know what Katherine herself has admitted to the archbishop?" she asked.

I didn't know the answer to Anne's question, but I suspected what it might be. To me, Katherine had stuck to the line that she had done nothing wrong. I believed that she placed such certainty in the king's love for her that he would ultimately take her word over her accusers'. For myself, I suspected that this stiff pride in the face of so much evidence would lead to her downfall, and that she would have been better advised to confess all and hope for mercy.

I told Anne as much. "But I cannot blame her for clinging on to this hope," I added, "or she would have certainly lost her reason and her mind."

"I fear that the king will never relent," Anne said, sighing. "They say that the fact he loved her so truly explains the betrayal he feels now."

There seemed little else to be discussed between us, and the wind was cold. After a final hug, Anne pattered off.

"Just a moment!" I called.

She turned back to me, hands busy rewrapping her head. "Who brought you here, Anne?"

She tucked in her chin to disguise her grin. There was a hint of rose in her cheeks, I noticed, as her dimples deepened. "Master Barsby, of course!" she said lightly. "Shall I take him a message from you?"

"Oh! . . . No, nothing from me, thanks."

But I wondered why she had not volunteered the information. And I wished I had not asked, because I now felt envious of their journey home together, back to warmth and safety and to some relief from the cares that made my head ache. Although I had felt that my duty compelled me to come here with Katherine, I had been left feeling more alone than ever in my life. When Anne's slight figure had vanished from sight, I watched and waited for a long time, just in case someone else should appear.

At length, shaking myself as if to wake from a daydream, I turned back to the grey abbey building.

Chapter 38

Don't Worry, All Will Be Well!

FEBRUARY 1542

S ome weeks later the order came that we were to travel to the Tower of London, once again by boat. By now I was so tense with waiting that it seemed almost a relief.

There had been absolutely no personal word or message from the king, although we had been sent fine clothes for Katherine to wear. Katherine took great comfort in this. I could see that she was thinking that the gift showed that she had not been forgotten.

On the morning of the journey, we sat silently in a room over the abbey's gatehouse. The nuns of old must have looked out of this window for approaching travellers in need of hospitality or paupers in search of aid. But now I was watching for figures in red.

Katherine was washed and clothed as best as I and the dressers I had drummed up from among the abbey servants could manage. It was so odd to me to see her careless about her appearance. This morning she was composed, although pale.

"Who's that?" Katherine asked from her place near the fire.

"*Shh*, only the servants bringing logs from the forest," I said, speaking soothingly as I might to a child. I was terrified that she would start her deranged howling once again. I could not bring myself to say that it was a column of troops.

"But they're coming up here!" she said, and indeed the steps were now loud on the stairs outside the room in which we waited.

"Don't worry, all will be well!" I said desperately. I went to stand behind her, my hand resting upon her shoulder as we both turned towards the door. Tears were already welling in my eyes.

"Indeed," she whispered, "I believe it. I know that my husband will forgive me, for he loves me. This will be his messenger at last." At that she looked up at me and smiled, and placed her hand upon my own. Her faith nearly broke my heart.

"Open up." A stern voice accompanied a tap at the door. I crept to the door to open it. Outside was the tall figure of a guard. He had that air of invulnerability that I remembered from the yeomen guards we had seen standing outside the king's rooms on our very first night at court.

He gave me no chance to speak at all or to negotiate any kind of humane treatment for the queen. He thrust a paper towards me. Without delaying for me to read it, he marched across the room to where Katherine lay in a heap in her cushioned chair.

When he took her arm, though, she suddenly became as tense and wild as a cat, clawing and spitting without words. But the room was now full of armed guards. Despite the desperate, horrible writhing of her body, they bundled her with ease down the stairs and across the gardens to the river.

I stumbled behind as best as I could, though the tears in my eyes meant that I could hardly see my way. One of them splashed on to the parchment in my hand. I didn't need to read it to know that it was a warrant for my cousin's execution.

Chapter 39

Why Would You Run the Risk?

We travelled down the River Thames and through the great city of London in bright sunlight. The weather was cold, but the glittering water made the city almost pretty, as if it were decked out in holiday clothes.

As maids of honour, we had made this trip many times, from Westminster to Greenwich, from Whitehall to Richmond, riding in the king's own barge, our watermen singing songs to us, and distant cheers floating across the water from crowds of watchers on the banks. Today, though, there was no one watching from the banks, and the watermen kept pace to the slow, heavy beat of a drum.

Katherine looked half dead, blindly turning her head from side to side, and I knew that she was still looking for a sign or message that the king had relented and had changed his mind about the need for her death.

"Of course, many noble men and women have entered here and lived," Katherine whispered to me as we arrived at the Tower. Despite their blank faces, I could tell that our guards were hoping Katherine would come quietly, and that they wouldn't have to manhandle her again like they had done at Syon. I took her arm, talking to her, reassuring her. I, too, did not think I could bear any more violence.

So we managed to get out of the boat and up the steps, to be received by the Governor of the Tower with a semblance of normality. He led us quickly to a fair chamber in the palace that nestled inside the Tower's horrible walls of hard white stone.

At the threshold, though, Katherine's hard-won poise temporarily lapsed. "This room!" she said, clutching my arm. "This is the chamber where

Queen Anne, Anne who was Anne Boleyn, that is, spent her last living night. They executed her out on the green just below."

"How do you know?" I asked, not because I disbelieved her, but because I thought it would be good to get her to answer questions rather than to give way to fear again.

"Because my husband the king told me so the day he showed me the Tower and all its fine guns," she said sadly. "And he also told me how deeply he'd been deceived by the vixen Anne Boleyn. I remember him saying, just here by the window, that he and I shared true love, not some strange enchantment as she had cast over him! He didn't know himself in those days. He doesn't quite know himself now."

The Governor of the Tower was now gesturing in servants, who brought with them ginger cordial and venison patties and some wrinkly black raisins of the east. They bowed shortly and left. I guessed that they had orders not to enter into any conversation with us. Once we were alone, we sat at the table to eat, again on my part for something to do, rather than because I was hungry.

"Do you remember our banqueting table we prepared at Trumpton?" I asked Katherine. I had noticed that she was fingering the dried grapes. "And do you remember how beautiful it was?"

"Oh, yes!" she said. "Those were happy days with the old duchess and Juliana and you and, of course . . . Francis."

"Katherine," I began more earnestly. I looked her full in the face so that, with some reluctance, she was forced to raise her head and look back. "What . . . why . . . how did matters stand with you and Master Manham?"

At this I lost her gaze, and it went back down to the table.

"I can understand that you liked him when we were young, before we came to court." I decided to battle on with my questions whether she would answer or not. "I liked him myself—all the girls did. But why would you run the risk of seeing him later, once you were queen?"

I knew Katherine well enough to work out what she was thinking as she prised the raisins, one by one, from their wizened vine. She was calculating whether the release of information could harm her . . . and she decided that it couldn't.

"Well, Carrots," she began. "You know that we were all coached and trained to get into the king's bed."

"No!"

I sat back in my seat, a little stunned by her boldness.

"Oh, yes," she said, almost with a smile in her voice. "You, personally, of course, did not like to believe such a thing; you thought you were too grand for it. But that was the message behind all our lessons. Think about it! How to dance, how to flirt, how to show off our bodies. Any one of us girls could have caught his eye, and our families, the Howards and the Camperdownes, did not care which of us it was."

"That's not true!" I said crossly.

"Really?" she said. "Has your own father never spoken to you about sleeping with the king?"

Of course her arrow had struck home, and she could tell by my lowered gaze that her guess had been correct.

"But to sleep with him is not enough," she said, leaning forward and warming to her subject. "A subject's duty, as the king's wife or mistress or even his bedfellow for a single night, is to give him a son! The one thing that he needs, that *England* needs. The king's son Edward is young and sick and likely to die. What the King's Highness requires — at any cost — is a baby boy."

She paused to let this sink in.

"But, Katherine," I said, "you never found yourself in the condition of being with child, and for certain the king was with you very often. We all know how much he enjoyed your company in the bedchamber."

"Exactly," Katherine hissed. She drew even closer to me, and I could smell the slight sourness of her breath. "It is treason to say it, but I believe that for all his love of frolicking, the king will never have a son. He . . . cannot act like a good husband should with his wife."

I sat still as stone, wishing that I had not heard this. It was treasonous to say something like this of the king, and if it were known by any other creature that I had heard her words, it could mean my death.

"Which is where Master Francis came in," she

continued. I believe she was enjoying my discomfort. "You noted, of course, the colour of his hair?"

"Indeed. It was red, like mine. Or like the king's." I spoke slowly.

"Indeed it was," Katherine said, "and his baby was likely to have red hair too. And Francis himself was well able to act as a man should towards his wife. For helping me with my great and sacred duty of trying to give the king a child, though, he was tortured, condemned, and put to death."

"You were planning to trick the king!" I cried. "To deceive him with Master Manham's baby! How could you be so . . . so wrong and so bold?"

Katherine looked at me—no, right through me—as if she were a hundred years old.

"I had no choice," she said tonelessly. "My family wanted me to catch the king. You knew that. Once I had caught him, I had to produce a baby or I would lose him. You think I took a great risk in trying to bear the baby of Master Manham . . ."

I stared back at her, dismayed.

"But if I failed to produce a baby, something I realised was impossible with the king, it would only have been a matter of time until I fell from his good graces. He would have moved on to someone else. I don't think I could have borne that. It was a greater risk to remain a good and faithful wife."

And now, for the first time, I think, I felt the beginnings of true pity for her. Throughout all her wretchedness of the last few weeks, I had felt sorry, yes, for her pain, but also I had felt that her behaviour had been uncomprehendingly selfish. Now, for the first time, I saw that she had been caught in a trap not entirely of her own devising.

We were roused by a tap at the door. Suddenly we were brought back to the present day and the horrible place in which we found ourselves.

The Governor of the Tower was back. This time, his servants brought in with them a strange lump of wood, perhaps a footstool. They laid it on the floor before us.

"My lady," he said, "here is the block. I have had it brought that you might practise laying your head upon it, as you will need to on the morrow."

As Katherine knelt on the floor, leaning forward and sideways to the block with her neck, it was like a strange and horrible parody of the dance we had made up at Trumpton Hall, the "Dance of the Gentle Fawn." I had hated to witness her twisting, spitting resistance to the guards earlier, but this was even worse. It was as if all the fight had gone out of her.

I could no longer bear it, and strange stars and storm clouds seemed to whirl and wheel across my vision. I had to rush out of the room. Sinking on my heels onto the dirty floor of the passage and resting there, I closed my eyes and hoped that the fainting fit would pass.

Chapter 40

Courage!

I'm not sure how long I spent there, squatting down on the floor, the chill of the stone seeping into my bones. It could have been minutes or hours. There was no room left in my heart for hope. It was so full of horror and despair.

Eventually I was roused from my reverie by the tapping of little feet in leather slippers. A tiny boy stood before me in the passage. It took me a moment or two and a blink or two to recognise him as the youngest of all the pages of the royal household. He was dressed in a doublet and hose like a man, despite being only about ten years old. At the end of the corridor, I saw a couple of yeomen bobbing their heads to me. I had been so lost in my own misery that I had not heard the door opening to let him in.

Slowly, I climbed to my feet, putting up my hands to smooth my hair. I was past caring that they had seen me on the floor.

The young page now made a careful bow, but I could see that he was trembling a little under the pressure of performing his duties. I could also see that he was holding out in his palm a folded letter. My heart leapt. A letter! This was the reprieve!

I grabbed it, speculated whether to take it in to Katherine or to read it first. But the boy was shaking his head, his chubby cheeks wobbling a little comically from side to side. "For you, m'm," he mumbled, unwittingly bringing back a memory of Little Em, who was now missing an ear.

"Thank you," I said huskily. My throat was painfully dry. I couldn't bear to wait until I was alone. I ripped the paper open with clumsy fingers.

In a second I was back on the floor, doubled up

in another fit of weeping. It wasn't the reprieve, but it was the next best thing.

The note contained just one word: *Courage!*

And it was in the hand of Ned Barsby.

Chapter 41

The Block

13 FEBRUARY 1542

The next morning, I felt that I was a century older and wiser than I had been the day before.

I had stayed all night by Katherine's bed, praying, talking to her in the moments when she was awake, and, at other times, simply looking at the wall and thinking. When it got too much, I lifted my head, looked out at the moon through the window, and remembered Ned's note. *Courage! Courage!*

Katherine, strange to say, did pass some hours asleep, and I think that she drew her strength from her belief that in the end her husband would still soften and commute her sentence to prison or maybe exile, like Anne of Cleves, the king's sister.

My misery was deepened by the realisation that I had wasted so many years hating Katherine. Now, when it was almost too late, I understood that I had been wrong to do so. She was not quite the conniving, grasping schemer I had always thought, anxious to take what others wanted.

Of course she had been ambitious and false and selfish, but our conversation had made me see the last few years in a new light. Of course the old duchess had been training us up to be bait for the king. We were just pawns in the game of winning more power for our families. If I had played the game a little better, it could have been me instead of Katherine in the Tower. And if I had played the game quite a lot better, I could have had the crown on my head and hopefully a baby in my arms.

It should not have been a surprise. After all, I had been told for as long as I could remember that I must do my duty for my family.

＊

Long before dawn, there were men and guards knocking at our door, demanding that we prepare ourselves. The priests were in and out, along with the lawyers. I was shocked by the absence of Katherine's relatives — I was the nearest to her in terms of blood, and everyone else stayed away. I knew that I was running a risk myself, of guilt by association, in remaining with her and serving her to the last. But I could not have left now for the world.

All of Katherine's tears and storms seemed to be over, and if she still expected the king's message of reprieve, she did not speak of it. I was the one who could not stop weeping.

With a heavy heart, I brushed what had been her lovely hair. So much of it had fallen out in the last few weeks that there was little left, and that I covered with her cap. I straightened her black skirt and finally took her in my arms and sobbed. She remained stiff as a corpse, looking over my shoulder, I could tell, as if she had already gone from the world.

The guards led us down on to the green below the window. It was hardly light yet, and a flaming torch helped us to find our footing on the stairs. A huddle of men in black stood around a small, low wooden platform, the scaffold. These were the official witnesses, lawyers, and priests.

Bearing herself like the queen she was, Katherine now mounted the platform. With dignity and poise, she knelt to say her prayers and to make a confession of all her faults to the priest. I now felt proud of her, proud on behalf of all the maids of honour, proud on behalf of all of us courtiers who knew how to smile in the face of pain, as she stood and looked at this great danger with such calmness and resolution.

Eventually, her prayers were done. She took off her cap and knelt before the block, just as she had practised the night before.

A masked figure, darkly dressed, detached himself from the crowds of waiting men and stepped up next to her. This, I realised, was the executioner, his face hidden so that men afterwards would not be able either to praise or condemn him for taking a woman's life.

I felt a strong grip upon each of my arms. The guards were trying to pull me back, to shield me from the sight. But I also felt that I should be there with Katherine for as long as I could. "Get your hands off me!" I hissed violently, so that they were forced either to make a noise and a disturbance or let me be.

And so, straining against the grasp of the guards, I watched as the executioner raised his axe against the dawn sky. I saw every tiny movement as he grunted and brought it down with a swift, almost graceful chop. Finally, I saw every drop of the blood that spilled from Katherine's beautiful, broken neck.

Chapter 42

He Needs You

MARCH–JUNE 1542

After the execution, I spent a few more days in the Tower, tidying up and disposing of Katherine's goods and letters and trinkets. During my time there, which I spent pretty much alone, I fretted about my return to the court.

Of course I wondered whether to return at all, whether it was better not to go back to Stoneton and consider the great game to be over. I could see more clearly than ever that Hampton Court, so glamorous, was full of fearful danger. But I wanted to see Anne and Ned and Will and the countess. They would sympathise with me over what I'd seen, what I'd experienced, whereas my father would not understand at all. And if I failed to return to court, I would face his wrath. Ultimately, I did not propose to risk that. I knew my duty.

I need not have been worried about whether I'd be welcome back at court. I was far from tainted by association with Katherine. My time in the Tower seemed almost to enhance my status. Once I had returned, and as life began to resume something more like its normal course, I began to understand that my fellow courtiers wanted — no, needed — a trusted witness to tell them about their former queen's end. One by one, they took me aside for a quiet word. Among them was the Countess of Malpas.

"And did she praise God and the king at the last?" she asked me out of the corner of her mouth. We were seated side by side at a feast, and the room was so noisy with drunken singing and laughing that it provided cover enough for her words. At this moment Will Summers, seated opposite us, chivalrously toasted me with a glass of wine, and I paused before replying in order to raise my goblet in return.

"Indeed, she died a Christian death."

Now the countess, too, was forced to pause in order to select a sweetmeat from the basket being brought around by Anne Sweet.

"And was there very much . . . blood?" she continued.

"Yes, there was a vast amount," I said, raising my fan and shielding myself behind it so as not to be observed, "and it entirely soiled and spoiled her black velvet dress and all her linen beneath."

The red raspberry tart the countess held in her hand looked so disgustingly shiny and sticky that it made my stomach heave.

"Ah, that's a great pity! You should have had the use of her left-behind clothes yourself."

Always the courtier, the countess sympathised with me over what would normally have been a major setback in a maid of honour's life: being cheated of an expected gift of cast-off clothing. She turned from me and bit into her tart.

The countess, and each and every questioner, left my presence, I felt, with a sense that the story of Katherine Howard had been satisfactorily finished.

The only person who asked me nothing was

Master Ned Barsby. As soon as I had returned to court, I asked where he was, for I was eager to see him again.

But Master Summers told me that Ned had gone from court. "Simple soul!" he said to me that evening, as we walked in the procession behind the king to chapel. "He went off without permission, meaning that he'll be in serious trouble if ever he tries to come back. Burnt his bridges. The king was quite cut up for two whole days."

"But where did he go?" I asked, tucking my hand into Will's elbow as we promenaded.

"Oh, I don't know," Will said vaguely. "The death of your cousin rattled him." We took another few steps, each of us nodding to the crowds of petitioners who lined the gallery whenever the king passed to chapel. "He couldn't really handle court life, you know. He was too honest. If you ask me, he'll marry that sweetie-pie friend of yours and they'll settle down in a cottage."

Will suddenly looked at me sharply, as if recollecting that this might be painful news. "Never mind," he said, patting my hand on his arm. "You've bigger fish to fry, my dear," he said.

It was true that my time with Ned seemed to belong to an age before the Flood in the Bible, and I had been only a child then. But the memory of his kind word in my darkest hour was fresh and vivid. The news that I would not see him again gave me such a pang that it was as much as I could do to keep putting one foot in front of the other and not to double up against the wall in pain.

But I had to walk on. "Really, Master Summers?" I said smoothly, adopting my best bland courtier voice. "That is most interesting news." My speech was so steady that he might have just confided in me his hopes that tomorrow would be a fine day.

Of course that's what Ned would do, I thought to myself, as Will Summers and I strolled onwards towards Mass. I had to steel myself, as I had done once before when I'd cut him out of my life. It had been weak and stupid to let him in again. Nothing must touch me ever again. *The note he sent me in the Tower was just typical,* I told myself. *Sentimental and naive.* Courtiers could not afford emotion, I said in my head. I could not afford emotion.

***

In the days that followed, I did what I could to burnish the court's memory of Katherine. I kept to myself the explosive information she had given me on her last evening alive and revealed nothing about Francis Manham's role in the tragedy. I always professed ignorance of her motives, although I was scrupulous to say that maybe we did not know all the facts. Master Manham himself was long since dead, from the horrible traitor's death of hanging, drawing, and quartering. I did not allow myself to think about this too much.

Instead I stressed that my cousin had faced her death with dignity, strength, and Christian belief, trusting in the goodness of God and the king. I did not describe her collapse and hysterics at Syon, only her stoicism and poise at the Tower of London. But despite my efforts, I knew that evil rumours were still circulating about all the misdeeds she was said to have done.

Perhaps the strangest conversation I had of all was with the king himself. When I was summoned to his chamber, I feared the worst and felt that my days must surely be numbered. He must have decided that the former queen's cousin was not to be trusted and was preparing to send me, also, to the Tower.

When I entered his secret, inner room, I found it lit only by the dim light of a low fire. In the gloom, I could see his great hulking body stranded on his carved bed like a whale washed up upon a beach. The hulk shuddered gently, and I perceived that the king was crying. As I drew close, I could see that his face was a horrible mess of tears and mucus. He held out a hand to me and made me sit down beside him on the feather mattress.

"I loved her," he said over and over again, as I felt myself beginning to weep once more. "She was my rose without a thorn."

I understood why Katherine had clung to her belief that the king would spare her, for his grief convinced me that he had genuinely felt a grand passion for her. "I wax old now," he snuffled. "She was the last love of my life."

Once again the contradictions of our master overwhelmed me. How could he send the woman he loved to the scaffold, yet be this distraught about doing so? But then the king had always been a romantic man. The deeper his love ran, the more violently he reacted when it turned sour.

I believe the king took some comfort from my presence — even though I was nothing but cowed, silent, and shaking — for he called me back again the next day.

I had to steel myself to bear the stench of his ulcer, as did everyone who spent any time in his chamber. When he wasn't lying on his bed, I had to watch him wolfing great slices of pie and gingerbread, washing them down with spirits and ale, as if he could find some comfort there in his food now that he was all alone in the world.

"All alone!" he would sigh, pouring himself another drink. "All alone, except for my fool and myself."

At that Will Summers and I would exchange glances as we stood waiting at the king's table, and make a mock bow and curtsey to each other.

Will Summers was another member of the select group of courtiers whose presence the king seemed able to bear. He, too, tried to make the hours pass, if not merrily, then at least smoothly and without paroxysms of royal tears.

During those hours I spent sitting with the weeping king, I had plenty of time to ponder on the strangeness of the situation. I gradually grew to understand that he didn't hate Katherine — he only hated what she'd done. And he felt that I had been a good friend to her and was therefore a good servant of his.

The situation was dangerous, but it was gratifying too. As I was so often in the king's chamber, the guards now simply nodded me in. At meals I was sometimes served even before the countess. I recognised that this was not an error but a concealed compliment from the Lord Steward. I knew that it was wrong, but it was almost impossible to resist the rising tide of pride that this brought me.

In the summer of that year, with Katherine dead and buried for some months, my father came down from Stoneton once more. The old Howard Duchess of Northumberland and Katherine's uncles were nowhere to be seen at court this season, as the power of their faction had been broken. But my father was riding high on the back of my position as the king's confidant.

When he called me to the gardens on the day after his arrival to walk with him and my aunt Margaret, I knew already what they would say. I understood all too well where my road led.

As I approached the bower where the two of them sat waiting for me, they knew, and I knew, that they need not speak at all. They were expecting, and all the rest of our family, and indeed the whole court was expecting me to take advantage of my opportunity. Two years after our first conversation on the topic, my hour had come at last.

"You, Rosebud," my father said. "It is your time. It is your turn. The king in his grief is vulnerable. He's lonely and sad. He needs you. Your family needs you. It is your chance to make yourself, and us, great. Take the hand that the king will offer and grasp it."

Chapter 43

The New Mistress

JUNE 1542

Two years ago, my father's suggestion that I should become the king's mistress had filled me with horror and dismay. Now, however, I had nearly twenty summers behind me. As well as a failed marriage of my own, I had experienced intimacy with the great King Henry the Eighth of England, and I had seen my cousin die in front of my eyes.

I was not shocked and did not cry, nor did I need to go running for help from Ned Barsby or Will Summers or anyone else.

In fact, now we had come to the brink, I felt nothing at all. I could see with the clarity of expensive Venetian glass the future that lay before me. If I followed in the footsteps of Katherine, my journey might end with great success and great riches. I could be queen. With careful arrangement, I could be the mother of a future king, and my family would be secure and overjoyed.

On the other hand, if I fluffed, I could fall. One slip, one false step, and I could end up on the block like Katherine. Perhaps I was already in danger. I might even now find it difficult, having come this far, to withdraw from the king's affection. I knew that he was starting to lean upon me.

That evening the king's chamber was dim and close, the air stale in my nostrils. I stepped forward and closed the door quickly, confidently, almost slamming it. Despite the gloomy, murky atmosphere of the room, I smiled.

I was buoyed up from the admiring glances I had received as I strode through the palace cloisters. I had observed the servants and courtiers I had passed admiring my green dress, tightly belted around my waist, my shining copper-coloured hair coiled up on the back of my head, my long, white throat, and my green, cat-like eyes.

Mistress . . . the new mistress. I'd heard the whispers in my wake. People recognised me. I felt deliberate and confident, almost like a queen.

And now, here in the shadows, lurching to his feet from his velvet chair, was the king himself, the great lumbering bear of a man. I could smell his sour breath from ten paces away.

"Ah, my green fairy!" he said. "Oh, you've come at last. Come and sit with me." He lowered himself — no, collapsed — onto the edge of his enormous ebony bed, crushing the fine furs upon it heedlessly under his massive weight. His leg must have been giving him pain again.

I curtseyed low, with grace and poise. I remained down upon the floor in my obeisance for a ridiculously long drawn-out pause. I stole a glance up through my lashes, then quickly returned my gaze to the floor. We both knew that this was just a sham of deference. He needed me, depended upon me, desired me. In this room, power flowed from me. He drank it up; he could not take his eyes off me.

At last he sighed.

"*Please* come and sit here," he said, patting the bed. His voice was lower than it had been and croaky. I had taken his breath away. Slowly I rose, savouring the moment, taking my own time. I took a slinky step, then another, towards the bed. I sensed that he was nervous, this great beast of a man of whom the whole world was afraid.

Tentatively, he put out a hand towards me.

I took it with a show of reluctance, looking away, still standing, still refusing to meet his eyes.

This gave him confidence. "Eliza!" he said huskily. He grabbed my arm and tugged me down to the bed beside him. His great paw of a hand dropped down lower—directly onto my thigh beneath the green skirt. I felt his breath on my cheek.

My heart almost stopped. All too soon, the moment had come. This was crossing a line. I stared at his hand, the hand of an old man, which now shyly moved up my leg.

I watched it. I waited to feel something. I had strived for this moment for years. I had steeled myself for it, trained for it. Hadn't I?

I sat there undecided as he slobbered all over my hand with his hot red lips. I remained still as a statue, either afraid or unwilling to draw back—I was not sure which. I don't know how far things would have gone, but the French ambassador was announced, and I took the first opportunity to leave.

"I shall see you later, Mistress Camperdowne!" were the king's last words as I hurried out.

Chapter 44

Why Does Everyone Think That
I Am in Love?

Later that evening I was slumped on my bed, alone in my chamber. I was supposed to be at the great court dinner, and my place beside my father would be empty. I knew that my absence would give rise to comment, but I felt so tired I could hardly stir.

I wanted time and solitude to think about this choice before me, but it felt like no choice at all. Every lesson in my life so far had prepared me to go to the king, take his hand, and offer him everything I had to give. I loosened my gown and kicked off my slippers. Feeling weary and immensely old, I leaned back on the bolster and stared up at the smoke-stained ceiling near the window. It was dirty, plain plaster, nothing like the wonderful gilded ribs and patterns in the queen's rooms.

Why, with success staring me in the face and the prospect of living beneath the best ceiling in the palace, could I think of nothing but the fresh wind of Derbyshire and the sound of the brook beneath my old bedchamber window? Why did I heave such a deep and loud sigh that it sounded almost like a sob?

I went to my window in search of a breath of air, something I had not felt for an age. In the courtyard below, I heard a chuckle. I glanced out, suddenly aware that my miserable face, lit below from my candle, must have been visible for all to see, for the panes stood wide to let in the gentle breeze of summer.

"You look a very picture of melancholy, Eliza!" It was a familiar voice.

Anne Sweet lifted the horn lantern she carried up near her face, so I could see it and confirm what my ears had already told me. I clucked my tongue with annoyance. In a palace, even to look out of the window was to broadcast one's private business to the world. I should have known better.

"Oh, Anne!" I said wearily. "Are you coming up?"

But she was already halfway up the stairs, and moments later I heard her scratch at the door. When I opened it, she was looking furtively each way along the passage.

"What's going on?" I asked, a little peeved at her histrionics.

She bustled forward into the room, a small smile playing around her lips, and made a great business of taking off the kerchief she'd had over her head.

"Now!" she said, plumping herself down on the edge of the bed to which I had retired. "I've come with some very important news. Come on, sit up and listen." She was snapping her fingers at me, which was uncharacteristic.

It would not have taken a fortune-teller to deduce that my thoughts were elsewhere, my gaze once again travelling over the dirty patch on the ceiling.

But something about Anne did catch my attention. She seemed to be full of fire.

"What is it, Anne?" I asked, turning my eyes but not my head towards her.

There was a pause, and Anne laughed gently.

"You look so sad, Eliza," Anne said. "But in my pocket here I have the very thing to make you happy."

It may have been my imagination, but the room suddenly seemed filled with the scent of rose petals.

"I've come with a message," she said.

I kept my face resolutely turned to the ceiling and flicked my eyes back to the vertical. "Please don't," I said tonelessly. "I don't want to see the king tonight. I'll have to send a message that I'm ill."

"No! No!" In her excitement, Anne jumped onto the bed and grabbed my shoulders, and I felt her warm breath on my cheek as she forced me to meet her eye to eye. "My message is from someone else altogether."

Now confusion and expectation must have filled my face, and I sat up to see her more clearly, sniffing back my tears.

"Master Barsby," she said slowly. "Ned. He wishes to marry you. You know that already, I think, don't you?"

I gasped. "But, Anne," I said weakly, hanging my head in amazement and mumbling down at my chest. "I thought that you . . . liked him yourself."

"I do," said Anne quietly. "But all he ever wants to do is talk about you."

I took this in, silently appreciating her generosity.

"But I know I can't think of him," I went on. "You know that if I marry, it has to be an earl. You know that as well as anyone at court!"

"It's not your duty to break so many of God's commandments," Anne said, "by lying with the king in his bed. You don't really want to do it, do you? And you shouldn't have to."

She sighed, and we both knew that my father would not agree. But he was old and weary. I flipped my head from side to side, still astonished at her words.

"You should marry for love!" Anne declared.

"Lord!" I snapped. "Why does everyone think I am in love?"

"Oh, Eliza, everyone knows it," she said, and now she was laughing again. "You may deceive yourself, but you cannot deceive the world. You are so brave.

You go into the lion's den and put your very head into his mouth. You can stand and look even the king in the eye. But you are too proud and stubborn and dutiful to admit that Ned is kind and good and loving, and more worthy of you than that old man, and that you love him back with all your heart."

"'That old man'?" I gasped at her heresy.

"Eliza," she said, "I'm not saying this for your happiness, though I believe that if you go away with Ned, you will be happy. I'm saying it for your survival. There is nothing for you here. You know what has happened to all five of the king's wives: cast aside or dead. Only by leaving now, immediately, can you escape Katherine's fate."

Now she had me. "But I can never leave," I said in a toneless drone, echoing words that Ned himself had said to me.

"Well, Ned has managed it," she said tartly. "And you can too. Here's the plan." Gathering herself together, she rose from the bed and grasped its post. At that moment I would have taken gentle Anne for the commander of an army.

"You, my dear, are about to succumb to a bout of

the sweating sickness. It's very virulent and very catching. You will not leave this chamber for some days. I will stay here and nurse you, of course, and meanwhile I will send your tiring woman, Henny, back to Stoneton to bring herbs and supplies."

"But it's a long way! Will Henny agree to go?"

At my words, the door swung open. I could see a familiar plump figure on the threshold, a big smile cracking her rosy face. Someone had been eavesdropping.

"Indeed, she will not go," said Henny herself. "You, Eliza, wearing a goodly number of gowns to increase your girth, will go in my place, pretending to be me. That's how you will escape!"

"I sense that sickness is coming over you, Eliza," added Anne in mock seriousness. She was almost shaking with delight and excitement and nerves. Henny was trembling too. They were proposing that we break just about every rule in the book, leaving court without permission and sneaking off in the night like thieves.

"You will need to keep to your chamber for many days for the protection of His Majesty's health,"

Anne went on, while Henny nodded sagely. "And I will guard your door like a dragon. I won't let anyone in to see that it's really Henny in your bed. In fact, no one will even try to come in if they think the sweat is here."

I was left speechless, swivelling my head between the two of them in wonder. Their certainty and complicity had me in its spell. Yet one thing dogged me.

"But does Ned . . . really . . . still want me? I have not been . . . kind to him."

"Yes, Eliza!" They spoke simultaneously.

"Ah, with all the excitement, I quite forgot," said Anne, plucking at her pocket and imperiously thrusting a much-folded piece of paper at me. "Here's the letter. He tells you himself."

Reluctantly, scarcely able to believe it, I unfolded the scrap of parchment. This time the message was much longer than one word. *Come, Eliza, and let me give you my heart*, it said. *I want nothing more than to live with you, and to love you, for the rest of our days.*

Down below my chamber, I could hear horses moving around and men speaking in low voices to calm them. Over in the Great Hall, I could hear the sound of musicians and the low distant hum of the palace. The courtiers were hard at work, feasting and flirting, busy with their own power play, paying no attention to our quiet courtyard.

I could scarcely read to the note's end because my eyes were full of tears. Through them, I dimly saw that Henny's arms were full of cloaks and dresses, as if she had come already prepared to bundle me up to impersonate her.

But Henny dumped the cloaks on the bed and beckoned me back out into the passage. "*Shh!*" she said sternly. "Come quickly and look." She was peering out through the window that looked the other way, not into the courtyard within but out towards the gardens rolling down to the river. Beyond the perimeter of the gardens, under the dark of the trees, she pointed out two dim shapes. Horses.

She gave a long low whistle.

Through the gloom I saw a figure step forward. There was the movement of a gentleman bowing low and sweeping his hat off his head. It was far too distant and too dark to see, but even so my mind filled in every detail of his wolfish smile. Ned was here! He was waiting for me!

So I should dress now as Henny and take an evening stroll in the gardens? It seemed so natural and normal, but it would take nerve. And yet, I could now be as bold and brave as my tiny toy knights. I felt utterly changed. Inside my chest, I could feel a warm steady glow, the glow of Ned's love and mine.

"Yes!" I said to Anne and Henny both, laughing and crying at the same time. "Help me! I'll get ready at once!"

But now that Anne had done her work of rousing me from my lethargy, I began to see just how nervous she was. She went to the courtyard window, staring and straining out, and letting us know whenever a guard went past on patrol. Meanwhile Henny was helping me to bundle up, both of us moving very quietly, but quickly, confidently. Finally, I was ready.

Henny gave me a huge hug. At that I almost melted and decided that it would be better to stay here and not run the risk of leaving.

"Go, Eliza!" Henny hissed. "Go now. He's waiting!"

Then Anne came over, and she, too, hugged me for a long time. "I owe you, dear friend," I said. "I can't tell you how much." I could tell that she was crying, but she gave me a shove towards the door.

By now it was very nearly dark, with just a glimmer of starlight by which to see. I crept along the passage, tripping over the hem of my unaccustomedly long gown.

Again I smelt that strange scent of roses.

It was time to commit myself. I gathered up my heavy skirts and started down the staircase. I was out now, in the courtyard, crossing the cobbles, nodding to the sentry on the gate, then running, running through the gardens and climbing over the wall, kicking out at my ridiculous skirt. And finally, Ned was reaching to help me down from the wall and laughing.

Within seconds I was in his arms, and he was kissing me. It felt wonderful and glorious. At last, I was where I belonged.

"You came!" he kept saying, amazed. "You came after all!"

"Yes," I said into his neck. "I'm sorry it took me so

long. I was confused. But I'd rather live on a sheep farm with you than be queen of all the world. I know that now."

I couldn't see his face, but I knew he was smiling. And I knew that we would never be parted that night and the next day and all the days to come.

Epilogue

Why I Wrote This Book

If you visit Hampton Court Palace today, you yourself can walk along the so-called Haunted Gallery that leads from the Great Chamber to the chapel. It has red silk hangings and is still lined with Tudor portraits of some of the people in this book: Henry the Eighth himself, his fool Will Summers, the monkey.

The ghost that's supposed to visit here at night is the white-dressed figure of Katherine Howard, running to the chapel to beg her husband, Henry the Eighth, to spare her life, exactly as she does in chapter 34.

There's a door leading off this gallery, which most visitors don't spot because it's disguised behind hangings. It leads to a staircase, which in turn leads to the office where I'm usually to be found working, because I'm one of the curators who look after the buildings and collections at Hampton Court. This ghost, then, has been sighted only metres away from the place where I spend my days. Sometimes when I walk down the Haunted Gallery, especially late in the evening, I think about Katherine's screams as the guards took her back to her lodgings.

Personally, I don't believe in ghosts, but I am interested in where ghost stories come from. And they often bear some sort of relationship to real historical events.

If you read the history books about Hampton Court, though, you'll see it firmly stated that the story of the ghost of Katherine Howard is complete nonsense. That's because the palace's geography dictates that the queen's rooms — where Katherine Howard would have been — were nowhere near the Haunted Gallery or chapel. And most history books don't have a good word to say about Katherine herself. Because she had more than one sexual partner, her execution is often explained as something that was almost her own fault. Historians have described her as a "good-time girl," as an "empty-headed wanton," and even as a "juvenile delinquent." The consensus is that she was a ditzy airhead.

A few years ago, one of our researchers at Hampton Court was looking into the "ghost story" of Katherine Howard, because we wanted to check the facts before installing a "ghost" of our own in the Haunted Gallery for visitors to see. Indeed, we now have one: a very subtle silhouette of a Tudor lady crossing what seems to be a window, which is in fact created by a hidden projector. Most people don't notice this projection of Katherine's figure crossing the light, but sometimes, when the palace is quiet, it frightens the living daylights out of a more imaginative visitor who catches sight of it out of the corner of an eye.

So this researcher of ours looked again at the plan of the palace, to check most historians' belief that it was impossible for Katherine Howard to get from her rooms to the Haunted Gallery. This is not as straightforward as it sounds because of the changes made to the building over the last four hundred years. But, on examining the sixteenth-century plan of the palace, she noticed that there was indeed a little staircase—"the Queen's Vice Staircase"—that led from the queen's apartments to the Haunted Gallery.

She was quite surprised at this and doubted herself. So she then wrote to a Famous Historian of Hampton Court Palace, asking, "Is it possible that you've got it wrong? Could the events that the 'ghost' represents really have happened?"

"No!" came the reply. "Katherine Howard could *not* have run screaming down that gallery. It's a silly story, anyway."

After she told me this, I looked at the plan myself, and I could plainly see that she was right, and the Famous Historian was wrong. It seemed to me that the Famous Historian hadn't looked at the facts dispassionately, and that he'd given himself away with his comment that it was a "silly story." I think that he didn't want to give any more credence to this silly story about a silly girl, and therefore looked at the palace plan with prejudiced eyes.

I felt quite annoyed by this on behalf of that girl who died nearly five hundred years ago. And as I learned more about the real Katherine Howard, the more annoyed I felt. She may have been young and foolish, but I felt that the odds at court were so heavily stacked against her that it was unfair that her lasting reputation should be as a silly little strumpet. What if there was something about her that we didn't know, something that could cast quite a different light upon her actions?

After thinking about this, I decided that I would write a new version of Katherine's story myself, and the result is this book.

Eliza is a made-up character, but many of the scenes and events — for example, when Anne of Cleves reveals that she doesn't know how babies are made — really did happen, and there are sixteenth-century documents to prove it. Eliza's home of Stoneton was inspired by South Wingfield Manor in Derbyshire, and her red hair borrowed from my two favourite indomitable redheads of the sixteenth century, Queen Elizabeth I and Bess of Hardwick.

Of course I can't prove that the story I've told in this book is the real story, the true explanation for Katherine Howard's horrible fate.

But then again, no one can prove it isn't.

Acknowledgements

My sincere thanks go to the people who helped me with *Maid of the King's Court*. They are all my colleagues, past and present, at Hampton Court Palace, Felicity Bryan, Catherine Clarke, Daisy Goodwin, Hannah Sheppard, Zoe Griffiths, and Deborah Noyes. But most of all I am grateful to my sister-in-law, Kersti Worsley, and dedicate this book to her.